Contact the Author

For information or for copies of this book, Pat Lynch can be contacted at:

- Website: **www.grampastories.ca**
- c/o L&A Financial Group
  200-1030 Upper James Street
  Hamilton, ON   L9C 6X6

Stories
I Like To Tell

J.P. (Pat) Lynch

iUniverse, Inc.
New York   Bloomington

Stories I Like To Tell

iUniverse books may be ordered through booksellers or by contacting:

This is a work of fiction. All of the characters, names, incidents, organizations, and dialogue in this novel are either the products of the author's imagination or are used fictitiously.

iUniverse
1663 Liberty Drive
Bloomington, IN 47403
www.iuniverse.com
1-800-Authors (1-800-288-4677)

ISBN: 978-1-4502-5622-3 (pbk)
ISBN: 978-1-4502-5623-0 (ebk)

Printed in the United States of America

iUniverse rev. date: 11/2/10

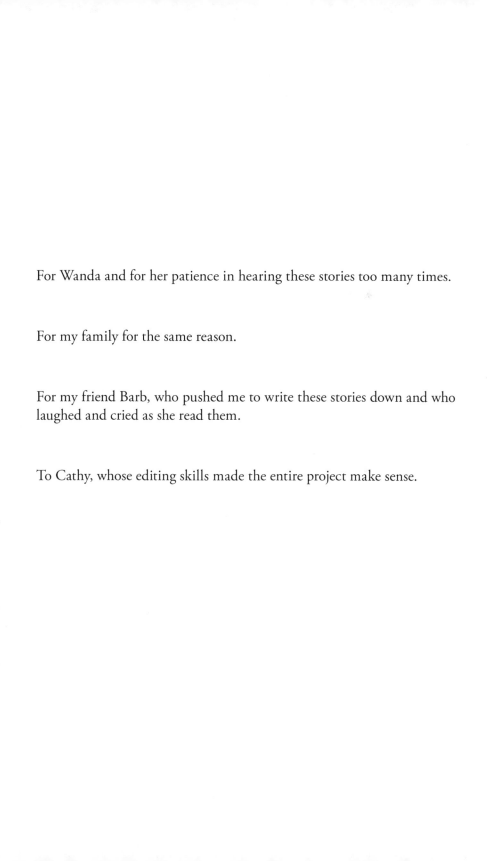

For Wanda and for her patience in hearing these stories too many times.

For my family for the same reason.

For my friend Barb, who pushed me to write these stories down and who laughed and cried as she read them.

To Cathy, whose editing skills made the entire project make sense.

Contents

Forward

I always liked telling stories and hearing stories. Over the years I had a number of things happen to me that turned into, what I thought, were amusing and sometimes interesting stories. I've enjoyed telling them and got the feeling that sometimes, people enjoyed hearing them.

There is no message involved in what I have put down. I tried to tell the stories on paper in ways that are similar to the way I told them in person. Most of the stories made me laugh. They made me laugh when they were happening. They made me laugh when I re-called them. They made me laugh when I re-told them. They made me laugh as I wrote them. Some made me well up just a little bit as old situations were recalled.

I started to write the stories at the urging of Barb and with the idea that the grandkids might read them someday and gain a little extra insight into grampa. It would be nice if some of my friends and family took a bit of enjoyment from them some day.

The stories are, for the most part, true and are based on my own experiences both good and bad. There is a little poetic licence taken from time to time and I confess to just a tiny bit of embellishment of some facts and circumstances. The names, in some cases, have been changed to protect the innocent.

One of my favourite Broadway plays was Camelot. One of the most memorable scenes came at the end of the play when a page was begging King Arthur to allow him to fight along side him the next day in the great battle. King Arthur refused and instead ordered the page to return to England and to tell everyone the story of Camelot. King Arthur, even as a myth, had it right.

Story telling is so important. I've often heard people regret that Mom or Dad or Gramma or Grampa never wrote down their stories. I just decided to write them down in case they were ever of any interest. It's been fun telling them. I hope those who read them and who know me can hear me telling them as you work your way along.

The old Irish language contains the word "craic". Craic is described as the type of happening, gathering or event that causes people to sit together and exchange tales, reminisce and enjoy the talk and stories of friends. In Ireland a good craic would involve an occasional Guinness or pop. Perhaps what I've done should be considered a contribution to a good old fashioned Irish craic.

Tell your own stories to others. It's called passing on lore and it's a good thing to do. I hope you have some fun with my collection of anecdotes and reminiscences.

Beagle Visit

When we moved into our first new house in Ancaster we were young and broke. We had selected an area that was beyond our means and we had bought a house for $15,000 with three mortgages. The house today would carry a value of close to $200,000. We like to believe that the increase in value was, in part, to do with the TLC we gave it when we were there.

We selected this particular house on this particular street because the person that I was working for at the time lived at the end of the street and because we knew some of our neighbours through an involvement I had with kid's baseball. One of the persons we knew lived across the street from our new home. They owned a really nice little beagle hound that they always kept fenced in and that slept in their basement whenever they weren't home.

The day we moved into our new house was particularly hot. We had worked from early morning and we were now sitting down among the boxes and packing crates enjoying a break and a cold drink. We had every window and door in the house open to catch whatever breeze we could. As we were totally out of funds, we had not purchased a storm and screen door for the front so it was sitting open to whatever flew or wandered past.

While we were sitting enjoying our break, lo and behold, what wanders through our front door, but the beagle. I knew Jack and Marg, the beagle's owners, were out for the evening so I was concerned that the dog had somehow managed to get out and was wandering around loose.

Being very fond of animals I wanted to prevent any harm from coming to the dog. Being the new kid on the block, I also wanted to make a good impression as the new neighbour. What a great opportunity.

I took the dog, which looked like every other beagle in the world to me, and walked across the street to Jack and Marg's house. The house was in total darkness. I didn't want to put the dog back into the back yard because I felt that if he found his way out before he would likely find his way out again and possibly get into trouble. It was lucky for that dog that it had wandered into the house of a person that cared.

The front door to the house was locked. The back door was locked. Fortunately, the side door that led directly into the basement was unlocked. I figured that is how the dog got out and the wind probably blew it shut after the escape.

I opened the unlocked door and let the dog loose in the basement. Immediately, the damnedest dog fight broke out that I had ever heard. Very obviously, Jack and Marg's beagle was already in the basement and I had just delivered a total stranger into his home.

As I knew there was no chance that I could ever sort out which beagle was which and as I had no need to jump into a dog fight in a darkened house, I took the only sensible action that could be taken.

I slammed the door shut and ran home.

Wanda and I decided, after I explained what had happened, that we had done quite enough unpacking for one day and that we were well advised to have our doors closed and lights out before Jack and Marg got home.

I know Jack and Marg wound up with only one beagle but I have no idea how they sorted it out or what their thoughts were when they got home and checked their basement. Obviously, you can't ask.

We moved three times after the initial move to Ancaster but I never again did anyone the favour of returning their dog unless the owner is on the other end of the leash at the time.

Building a Patio

My father died when I was fourteen. We lived on Prospect Street in a house that had been renovated so that it contained two small apartments as well as living quarters for our own family. We still only had one bathroom, which meant that before you took a bath and tied up the bathroom for any length of time, you first surveyed everyone in the house to make sure they had the opportunity of using the facilities. Any idea of having a long soak in the tub was dispelled by the rattling of the bathroom door knob. To this day I take showers.

The maintenance and management of the house fell to me. My skill level with maintenance items or building work was never very high and never improved as I got older. My friend Ted, on the other hand, loved carpentry and wood work and is darn good at it. I once asked him to help me build a wall to enclose our laundry room. After two sessions of putting up with my assistance, which meant allowing me to hold the dumb end of a board while he sawed, or occasionally sending me up to the garage to bring him a two by four, ended with him showing up with an odd looking device. I asked him what it was and he explained it was a device that held two pieces of wood together while he took the next step. He didn't need me to hold either piece. I realized then that I had been downsized in favour of a clamp. It was not my most shining moment.

At any rate, I did my best to keep things going at our Prospect Street house. I left school at age sixteen and bounced around from job to job before I settled in as a timekeeper/office manager for a construction company named Western Pile & Foundation Company. I am living proof that working for a construction company doesn't mean that you know much, if anything, about construction.

We had a small back yard and I decided it would be a nice touch to make a patio area out of coloured concrete slabs. I arranged to buy the slabs from a supplier close to Toronto and set out with Wanda in a borrowed pick-up truck to bring them back to Prospect Street. I had no idea what effect a ton and a half of patio stones would have on a half ton pick up truck. We discovered, if you put a ton and a half of patio stones in a half ton pick up truck the front wheels of the truck barely touch the ground. Even though this provides the feel of power steering, it is not a good thing.

We arbitrarily reduced the size of the patio design and unloaded patio stones to the point where the front wheels of the truck were once again touching the ground. Then, being the clever devils that we were, we put several stones in the cab with us in the belief that they would keep us better grounded.

There is an old story about a reward being offered to whoever could extinguish an oil well fire that had been burning for quite some time. Many had already tried and failed. Pete's Construction Company arrived on the scene in a pick-up truck. Without the slightest hesitation the truck rolled straight down the hill and rolled right over the fire area. The truck was blown straight up into the air just as Pete jumped out. By some miracle the truck landed right back on the fire, still upright, and the back-blow put out the fire. When asked what he intended to do with the $10,000 reward he had just earned, Pete replied that the first thing he was going to do is get the brakes fixed on his truck. I thought a lot about that story as we nursed our patio stones home.

The patio got built and actually looked quite good. It soon became apparent, however, that I had made a couple of serious miscalculations. The patio was situated so that it took the full blast of the hot sun all morning through to about two o'clock in the afternoon. It was impossible to sit out and enjoy it during that time. It was also situated so that it was under the very end of the branches of a big old maple tree that blocked the sun from the west but offered perfect perches to large number of birds that took the shade of the tree in the hot afternoons. Birds being what they are, their presence made it impossible to sit out and enjoy the patio during that time either.

We obviously needed an overhead shelter and I was the man to build it. I dug holes for four by four posts on each corner and for an interim post on either side and one in the middle at the front of the patio. I nailed two by four stringers connecting the posts and ran two by four stringers at three foot intervals across the shelter and at three foot intervals running from back to front. The entire set of lattice work was connected to the back of the house and sloped to the front of the patio. I then stretched a canvas tarpaulin across the entire top and tied it down to the side and front stringers.

It wasn't real pretty but it worked. I sat out there reading and enjoying life for the most part of the next week-end. It was good to be in the construction business. It was good to be handy and innovative. It was good to benefit from the work done with your own hands.

That Sunday night it rained. And it rained. And it rained.

Monday morning, freshly dressed for work, I looked up at my shelter while on the way to my car. I immediately made some observations and reached some conclusions:

-Water, including rain water, weighs a lot.

-Canvas, when weighed down by rainwater, stretches a lot.

-Two by four boards, when trying to hold up canvas weighed down by rainwater, bow a lot.

-My shelter had obviously lost its structural integrity and, if I didn't get some weight off, it could come crashing down and kill somebody.

As I had not yet made a lot of smart moves building my patio and the shelter, it shouldn't come as a big surprise that I continued to make bad decisions. I found a solid steel rake and used the end of the rake to push against the tarpaulin in an effort to move the water from one sagging pocket to the next lower row. The system was working. I had problems, however, repeating the process as more and more water collected in the lower set of pockets. By the time I had moved the water down to the last row, I saw that the tarp was sagging very dangerously. I could no longer hold the rake handle and make any progress lifting the water with the steel end of the rake.

I reversed the rake, figuring I could use the handle to push against the heavy pocket of collected water in a smaller area. I thought as the handle broke through the tarp, "I just made another big mistake."

The next thing I knew, I was wearing approximately twenty gallons of rainwater that was mixed with leaves that had already started to rot and with several days of bird droppings. I was late for work that day. I had a really good excuse but I couldn't tell anyone.

The shelter was torn down the next day and I gave up patio sitting. I went by the old place the other day and the patio stones are still there. Like the pyramids, some things were built to last forever.

Heroes

It's been said that you can't possibly know a person unless you know their heroes. I believe that statement, as a person's heroes tell you more about themselves than almost anything else. If you don't have heroes you may be missing a valuable guideline in your life. If you don't understand why you have selected certain persons as heroes, you should look into it.

I've marked down a few heroes over the years. Harry S. Truman because of his straightforward attitude and basic honesty is high on my list. George Patton because of his "get on with it approach" and his feeling that "it's better to go with a good plan today rather than try for a perfect plan tomorrow", philosophy. I liked the loyalty shown by Robert E. Lee when he chose his southland over the offered leadership of the northern armies during the American Civil War. He didn't agree with their cause, but he knew it was his home.

My only sports hero has been Ted Williams. He did his job. He played his entire career with one team. He twice answered military call ups and served his country without a word of reproach, even though the call ups carved huge holes into his playing career and cost him money and records. He kept the media out of his own life. Only Tiger Woods has been anywhere near as successful during the height of a playing career. He supported the children's Cancer Jimmy Hospital outside Boston for years. He would visit any kid that wanted to see him if the child was in serious health with the only proviso being that the visit be kept private and that the news media not be told. Why not have him on a hero list?

Terry Fox is high on the list. Thomas More has been one of my favourite historical heroes.

For several years I have attended the local B'nai Brith sports dinner. It's a big local event. It honours local high school athletes and it is the place to be seen with the movers and shakers of Hamilton. My friends, Larry and Marnie, always arrange to have me sit at their table and they often have very interesting guests along with them. Dan and I have attended the last several and it's great fun.

One year they had George Grant, a part owner of the Hamilton Tiger-Cats, as a guest at their table. I got talking to George during the dinner and commented that the Tiger-Cat stores did not carry enough paraphernalia for young kids. I told him that I made this discovery when I went shopping for something for my grandson Adam the previous Christmas. We agreed that the young kids are vitally important to the success of professional sports franchises as they are the fans of tomorrow. He asked Adam's age. Adam was ten at the time.

Before the evening was over, George had given me his card with his private phone number and told me to call him during the next season and he would arrange to get Adam and me on the field before a game and set it up so that Adam could meet a few of the players.

The next season I picked a game and called George Grant. Much to his credit, he remembered the conversation and the commitment. He arranged to have Adam and I meet him an hour before game time and said he would set it up for us.

I don't know which one of us was more thrilled. George was true to his word. We were on the field. Adam shook hands with a number of players. He had his picture taken with some of the starters. He was introduced to two former players that were having their numbers put up on the Tiger-Cat wall of fame. We were invited into the former players lounge where I introduced Adam to Cam Fraser who was a personal friend. He collected autographs from players that were from my era. We were invited into the executive lounge at half time. What a deal.

The Tiger-Cat fans have always had fun with a legendary cheer leader named Pigskin Pete. Pigskin Pete wears a bowler hat and a replica of the original Tiger Football Club sweater. He leads the fans in the old cheer, "Oskee-wee-wee! Oskee-waw-waw! Holy Mackinaw! Tigers, eat 'em raw!" which is probably the worse cheer in the annals of sports except for the Toronto cheer- "Yea Argos."

At any rate, Adam loved the game. He really liked the idea that you could look at the scoreboard any time you wanted to check the score and you needn't depend on a radio or television announcer for that kind of information.

At halftime we went into the executive lounge and, while Adam went to the washroom, I found a place at a table with Pigskin Pete. We were just sitting there with a cold drink eating popcorn and talking about the things people talk about at football games. Adam saw us there and joined us, finished his drink and just sat, listened and looked around.

He was a little more quiet during the second half. I think he was running out of gas. It had been a big night for him. When we were walking back to the car after the game and talking, Adam told me how great the whole event had been. He told me that it had really impressed him when he came back into the executive lounge and found his grampa "just carrying on a regular conversation with Pigskin Pete". Wow.

I think for that moment anyway, I was a hero to a ten year old. Yeah. Wow.

Telephone Calls

When my father was very ill we learned that a telephone call late at night never meant good news. I carried that feeling with me as an adult. This probably led to the house rule with our kids that they are to tell their friends not to call after 9:00 PM and to definitely not call early in the morning.

An early telephone call on a Saturday or Sunday morning was really frightening. This attitude changed somewhat as golf moved up the interest list and an occasional early morning call is now acceptable. "Occasional" is defined by me and that definition can change without warning.

I spent over twenty-five years in the construction business. The off hours telephone call is particularly frightening when you are in the construction business and your crews are working over-time or on night shifts. You never get good news calls in off hours.

Wanda was always very considerate in protecting me against such calls. One time our phone went off at 2.30 in the morning. It was a neighbour and friend. Wanda answered the call and her lady friend said to her: "Wanda, can I talk to Pat?"

"Is this really important?" asked Wanda. This is a 2:30 AM question.

"I think so. My husband has just had a heart attack and I don't know what I should do."

Under the circumstances, Wanda let me take the call.

One Sunday morning I was sitting at home, minding my own business, and the phone rang. We were working on a difficult construction project at a steel mill at the time that involved several heavy pieces of equipment including cranes and barges. We were shut down for the week-end so I wasn't concerned about work but I knew, instinctively, that a Sunday morning phone call couldn't possibly be good news.

"Hello" from me.

"Is this Mr. J.P. Lynch?"

"Yes".

"Is this the Mr. Lynch that owns Westpile Construction?"

"Yes", I knew this was not going well.

"This is Joe from Steel Mill Security. Do you have a crane on a barge down here at the bayfront?"

This is really not going well. "Yes, why?"

"Well" said Joe from Steel Mill Security, "the barge sunk."

Joe was obviously a man of few words. There was no warning. There was no lead in. There was no caution that I might wish to sit down for his news. There was only the three word sentence, "the barge sunk".

Every now and again we all find ourselves with brain cramps. At such times we invariably find that our mouths work much more quickly than our brains. I call it my talking out loud when I should be thinking voice. When it kicks into action it is very scary.

I then heard my talking out loud when I should be thinking voice asking Joe from Steel Mill Security, "Did the crane sink too?"

Joe, for some reason thought that he had just heard the most idiotic question ever posed including those asked in the British and Canadian Parliaments and the U.S. Congress. I, on the other hand didn't think it was quite so funny.

The only thought running through my head as I heard the question being asked was, "please God, make it not be me that I hear asking that question."

After several days of recovery work, two lawsuits and a major insurance claim that led to a court case, the crane and the barge were recovered. My stock at the Steel Mill went way down but my question made me a legend in the Security office.

The moral of the story is that you should always try to have the brain kick in at least three seconds before the mouth starts. It's good advice but it's seldom taken.

Driving in Boston

I spent some time in Sorel, Quebec keeping records on a caisson project for the old pile driving company based in New York City. The company had acquired a test project that involved attaching electrodes to the outside of a steel pipe casing that, in turn, drew water to the outside of the pipe and that, in turn, reduced the friction between the pipe and the ground and allowed for a faster and easier driving of the caisson pipe. Got it?

If the answer is "no" you are in line with the Harvard based soils experts that also didn't understand what they were trying to do.

We installed one caisson using the fancy electrode method and we installed one caisson right next to it using conventional driving methods. My job was to record the minute by minute and foot by foot progress of both and prepare a comparison report for our New York office. I very carefully kept the records and concluded that there was absolutely no difference between the two.

When I submitted my reports to the New York office I was summonsed to explain how I got it wrong, because the experts at Harvard said that the system worked perfectly in their laboratory. I was then sent to Boston to meet with the people at Harvard where, I think, I was expected to recant. Unfortunately, no matter how many times I looked at the records I concluded that method #1 took eight hours and forty three minutes to complete and method #2 took eight hours and forty three minutes to complete.

As these conclusions brought the consulting contract to an abrupt end and as I was the bearer of the bad news, I was dispatched without thanks. As a result of this particular episode I have been able to tell people that I had indeed, attended Harvard. When pressed, I also will admit that it was only for one day.

I was twenty-four years old at the time and the idea of being sent to Boston by a firm based in New York to meet with professors at Harvard was pretty heady stuff. The meetings were scheduled for Monday so I drove to Boston on the weekend and took Wanda, my mother and Tammara, who was barely a year old, along for the ride.

Boston is an old city with narrow streets that often change into other streets without any rhyme or reason. The drivers are all in an incredible hurry and they take you into the various poorly marked circles, then blow their horns frantically at you because you have no idea where you are or how you might get to where you're going. Add to that muddle, a driving rain and darkness and you get the picture of me trying to get out of the city with my entire family on board.

At one point I was trying to move over from one lane to another in a traffic circle when an even more urgent horn blowing started behind me and I realized I had started to move under a semi-trailer driving beside us. Boston may be filled with bad and discourteous drivers but a good one probably saved our lives that night. The experience kept me out of Boston for a long time.

After another twenty-two years of trying to screw up my courage, Wanda, Dan and Vickie and I decided to go to Boston to see the Red Sox. Vickie was probably the major influence in making the decision. She was always a big baseball fan and liked the idea of seeing a game at Fenway Park. It was a great trip without driving incidents. It was a very special trip because Vickie informed us that in a few months we were to become grandparents. Special things seem to take place in special places. This announcement and the subject matter, Katie, made Boston a particularly special place to us.

Another fifteen years went past. The Red Sox still never won a pennant. The city named a new tunnel after Ted Williams. A former Boston resident who became President, was assassinated in Dallas. Carl Ystremski was elected to the Baseball Hall of Fame. Larry Bird retired from the Boston Celtics and they stopped winning championships. The entire city had been disrupted by the "Big Dig". Arthur Fiedler had long since retired as conductor of the Boston Pops Orchestra. The FBI was continuing in their investigation of corrupt contractors.

On the other hand, tourists still walked the Boston Commons. The Fourth of July Independence Day concerts still drew millions, either in person or as TV viewers. Cheers was still open but Cliff Claven and his pals had moved on. The Old Oyster House restaurant still served the best seafood on the eastern seaboard. Traffic was still brutal and made worse by the disruptions caused by the "Big Dig" but I was once more brave enough to drive to Boston.

Wanda and I attended a conference being held in a waterfront hotel and conference centre. We crossed the Massachusetts border and discovered Stockbridge, which is the former home of Norman Rockwell, the painter. Take a few hours, if you are ever in the area, and go there. You'll love it. We also discovered an information centre that provided us with a map of the city of Boston with specific directions to our hotel. This was a major find and increased our confidence tenfold. There was now a reasonably good chance that we could actually find our destination on our intended day of arrival. This, for me, would be a major accomplishment.

With Wanda as navigator, three maps and a set of written instructions plus notes taken when I made the hotel reservations we were well into the city without too many problems. The traffic, however, was as we remembered it.

We were watching for a particular turn-off into a particular tunnel. We found it at the last second. I found myself in the far left lane of three lanes moving at fairly high speed. When we came out of the tunnel we made two discoveries; our hotel was one block down the street on the right and there were now three additional lanes of traffic merging to our right so that we were in the far left lane with five lanes of traffic to cross within a block. We also discovered that if we missed the hotel turn-off, our next turning point was somewhere in Vermont. It was time for aggressive optimism.

I started to edge over into the fifth lane on my right. Horns and fist shakings! I made it.

I started to crowd over into the fourth lane. More horns and more fist shakings! I made it.

I made it into the third lane but we were running out of block and our hotel was coming up fast. I threw on my signal light and cut straight across into the second lane, hit the brake and cut sharply into the curb lane. We made the hotel cut-off with six feet to spare.

Okay, there was some additional horn blowing and some extra fist shaking. So there were a few people yelling something about &%@#%

Canadian drivers, whatever they are, but we were out of the traffic and out of the car.

We were greeted by the hotel doorman. I handed him the keys and said, "Take these and hide them. I don't want to see this car for the next four days."

"The next time I see the car" I told him, "it will be to take the most direct route out of town. I also expect that I will be getting some kind of recognition as an honorary Boston driver in view of what I just went through to get across six lanes of traffic."

He just laid on a big Boston grin and with that great New England accent said,

"No sir. No Boston driver award for you, honorary or otherwise. I was watching you cross that traffic and you used your signal lights. That disqualified you as a typical Boston driver."

I still love Boston and I still believe the Red Sox will, one day, win a World Series.

Stearman

Over the years our daughter Linda has been very inventive with birthday gifts for those in the family, especially for her father. Too often we wimp out on gifts and we provide things that are safe and easy to buy. The wimpiest of all is the gift certificate. It may be appreciated by the recipient and it may be a smart purchase but it also tells the giver and recipient that you may not know enough about each other.

Wanda once took a gold pocket watch that had belonged to my father and had it set on a stand and gave it to me for Christmas. Restored pictures, poems from the kids or grandkids, the works of Robert Frost or Churchill diaries found in old book stores are all great gifts. Paul and Laura gave me a photo of yours truly at the helm of a sailboat. It was a great gift and it came at a time when I especially valued and needed their friendship. A bottle of single malt scotch works well.

I spent my 65th birthday in Ireland. Before we left on the trip I gave my three kids things that I particularly valued. I gave Dan my father's ring that I have worn since his death when I was fourteen. I gave Linda the gold watch and stand. I gave Tammara two pieces of scrimshaw that I got in Hawaii and that I've always loved. I was just looking to give a special gift on a special occasion. I told them I intended to keep them in use for a while but I thought they were good gifts and would make good memories. A thoughtful gift feeds the soul.

Linda gave me the gift of a canoe trip down the Grand River from Paris to Brantford. Linda and I shared the trip with Dan and my friend Larry. The Grand River wends its way through a very heavily populated area of Ontario but its banks, through the area we travelled, are primarily open to farm fields and forest. It's hard work against the wind but it's a beautiful trip. We once watched an air show from the deck of a boat in Toronto Harbour, another great gift.

When we were in the catering business we put together and served a banquet in the War Plane Museum in Mount Hope. The meal and tables were set out among the old planes. The disk jockey played Vera Lynn songs. It was a great atmosphere, a good night and a good party.

Sometime later I got talking with a client who was an ex RCAF pilot during World War II. He told me about learning to fly in an open cockpit aircraft known as the Stearman. He graduated to flying Lancaster bombers before he was grounded for making one too many questionable landings. I knew they had both those planes at the War Plane Museum and that they both still flew. From time to time we would see and hear the Lancaster flying circuits over the city of Hamilton. I never thought of airplanes as killing machines or of their preservation as an act of glorifying war. They were a reminder of a very difficult time and I loved the sound of their piston driven engines. Jets are impressive but the War Plane Museum Spitfire conjures up pictures of the pilots that used them to tip buzz bombs away from London during the blitz. They were special people.

My next door neighbour worked at the War Plane Museum as a volunteer. He pulled wrenches and helped restore and maintain some of the old planes. I found out, through him, that you could arrange a flight on the Stearman. I must have mentioned it around the family and the next thing I knew, Linda had arranged a flight for me as a birthday gift. Wow!

I booked the flight and also arranged flights for Linda and Dan to join me. Tammara was working out of town at that time and missed a great experience. We had been advised to have a particular pilot, John, take us on the flight. John was an ex military pilot who had retired on a pretty good pension. He then flew commercial jets for a number of years and retired from that job with a pretty good pension. He now spends his days flying guests in vintage aircraft.

It was a beautiful sunny morning. I went up first as the guest of honour. John provided a leather flight jacket and leather helmet for atmosphere. I sat in the front seat. John explained the controls and the radio and we were up and away.

I felt like a cross between Billy Bishop and my mythical hero, Snoopy from Peanuts. I felt I should be saying things like, "curse you Red Baron." John explained how to make the aircraft bank and turn. He actually let me fly the plane, his hands were tightly on the controls as well, and we made a couple of circuits over our nearby golf course. My golf pals were out there somewhere and I had alerted them to watch for a character in a yellow bi-plane. It was a major rush.

Dan flew next. Dan is usually quite non-plussed but he also remained ten feet off the ground after he had landed.

Linda flew third. She was a little nervous about the endeavour now that it was right in front of her. Both she and Dan refused the leather helmet. I guess they didn't agree with my assessment that Snoopy looked cool.

Linda was up a little longer than either Dan or me. As she started out a little nervous, we were anxious to see how she felt about the whole thing. The plane taxied to a stop. John climbed down, then offered his hand to Linda. Linda climbed out of the plane then immediately threw both her arms around John and kissed him.

John had the look and manner that you would expect from an ex military fighter pilot. He kissed back and said, "What a great country. I've got two pensions. I fly what I want when I want to and I get to kiss pretty girls. What a great country."

We turned in our gear, John presented us each with a certificate indicating we had flown a Stearman. Mine sits in my office along with a copy of the poem "High Flight" that I have had for years. The poem attempts to explain the feeling of flight as told by a young man who died in the war.

That poem starts with the words, "Oh, I have slipped the surly bonds of earth" and ends with the words, "Put out my hand and touched the face of God."

I was given a gift, and was able to share it, that gave me just an inkling of what Lieutenant Gillespie, aged 19, felt when he wrote that poem. Thanks.

No One I Would Care to Meet

Brian entered university when he was sixteen years old. His entrance year coincided with the year in which large numbers of World War II veterans were returning from the war and taking advantage of the university entitlements given to veterans. Brian, therefore, found himself sitting in classes as a wet behind the ears kid with some very jaded and battle-scarred war vets.

My friend was obviously clever beyond his years or he would not have found himself in that position. Having found himself in that position, however, it's understandable how he could have been somewhat traumatized by the experience. I always thought that the experience explained some of the ways Brian handled things in life. I learned otherwise.

He could bring a degree of concentration to anything he did that was especially enviable. All extraneous noises and activities could be almost completely, and I repeat "almost", block out all outside distractions as he went about his problem solving endeavours. He was always very confident about what he did, how he did it and how the situation would play out but, to those of us who spent time with him, it appeared that it hadn't always been completely thought through. There seemed to be that area in his mind that didn't quite leave him totally comfortable with where he was going. Over the years, I concluded that he must have suffered from some significant trauma.

For example, playing golf with Brian and other friends, we found ourselves betting on who would be buying the drinks and lunch at the halfway house during a round. Brian had a three foot putt that would get him off the hook if he made it or that would stick him with the tab if he missed. You could see the gathering of the powers of concentration as he lined up his shot. You could see him very effectively shutting down all outside noises and distractions as he assessed the slope and speed of the green. He double checked the wind velocity. He triple checked his stance and position over the ball. He had the rest of us, almost and I repeat almost, shut out.

Seconds before he was to make the putt, I commented quietly but within Brian's earshot, to one of the other players-

"It's muggy today."

"Yes" responded the other player, "today is muggy, followed by Tooggie, Weggie, Thurgie and Frigie."

We then watched Brian trying not to hear what was said and trying not to let it into his head or otherwise effect what he was trying to do. We then watched the total disintegration of his concentration abilities. We watched him hit his three foot putt approximately five feet. Brian was always very careful about his language but at that point, knowing that we knew he couldn't keep us out of his head, he resorted to his most violent language and to the dismay of us all, in a very loud voice said, "Blast".

Brian was a man who was never afraid to take up a cause when he felt it was right to do so. He taught me, to the chagrin of others including Wanda, that you could cause a greater stir over an issue by writing a letter to the President of the company, or the club, or the United States for that matter. In many ways he could be referred to as The Keeper of the Great Seal as he set out positions he thought were right and important.

While driving with Brian on the way to a fishing trip with two other fisherman friends, we passed through the town of Burks Falls. We stopped at a gas station to refuel and to pick up some snacks. The gas station had a rather large cage out the back and there sat a very plump and glossy coated black bear. This type of thing was quite common throughout northern Ontario. It's a practice that has long since been stopped but, at the time, it was fairly common to see such a situation.

This particular area was large and clean and housed what appeared to be a very contented bear that spent his days snoozing or accepting ice cream cones from visitors.

When we returned to the car, Brian was quite upset over the fact that there was a bear held captive in the cage.

"What do you think should be done about it?" we asked.

"The bear should be set free" he replied "and left to forage like bears are meant to do".

We argued that there is a substantial and successful bear hunt every year in that part of the country and that the bear had a much longer life expectancy at the Burks Falls gas station than he would have in the forest. We pointed out that they were shooting bears at the local town dump.

Brian still felt we should start a petition designed to "free the Burks Falls Bear". He admitted, when pressed, that the bear would probably not sign such a petition because the bear had thought it through further than Brian. The bear had a nice clean home, good food and an endless supply of ice cream cones supplied by passing tourists. Brian's scheme would leave him scrounging at the town dump and ducking bullets fired at him by beer drinkers.

This is not a commentary on proper zoo conditions or on proper management of the environment. It's simply an illustration of how a very intelligent person could put someone or something at risk because of a think void that occasionally pops up. Psychologists would point out that such things often skew thinking and are often caused by some past life trauma.

Brian was obviously driven to want to do the proper thing. He once got quite agitated when we walked to a drive-in restaurant. To him, there was something inherently wrong with being at a drive-in without a car. Somewhere, in his distant past, he had learned that the right and proper thing overwhelmed all else. One day I learned where and how the young Brian had been traumatized.

His father had come from a good and successful family. Dad himself had been a successful mining engineer who had lived in several different areas of the country as his work took him from place to place. Brian told me of being taken to the Empress Hotel in Victoria, British Columbia by his very prim and proper grandmother. They were to attend at the very formal high tea for which the Empress Hotel is famous.

Brian was an over-dressed and over-awed eight year old in a room full of fancy dishware and even fancier people. His grandmother was a tall, severe looking, furled umbrella carrying, white haired lady with a significant hearing problem.

Brian relates that his grandmother sat on the edge of her chair, her back ramrod straight with her hands resting on the top of her umbrella.

She looked around the room filled with Victoria society persons and an occasional visitor to the city and said in that extra loud voice that is often used by persons who are hard of hearing,

"Brian, I don't see a single solitary person in this entire room that I would care to meet."

Every sound in the room stopped and all eyes swung onto a dowager grandmother and an eight year old boy.

This is the childhood experience that must have scarred the poor lad for life. I think it explains the loss of concentration at critical moments. It probably explains the fear of being trapped in the wrong place at the wrong time. It probably explains the need to set a happy bear free, even if it is at great risk to the bear.

It was probably the first time in fear and anger that Brian said "Blast". It certainly explains why Brian has never been back to the Empress Hotel.

Detention

When he retired from his career position he was the CEO of one of Canada's largest and most successful corporations. He had worked his way through the ranks and earned every step forward. He was the Chairman of the Board at a major University. He was on advisory councils for the Premier of the Province. He was a great father and a great husband. Those who knew him held him in the highest esteem.

He was also my best friend.

The problem that he has always had with me is that I knew him when he was just a kid. We played sports together. I dated his sister. He introduced me to the woman that I fell in love with and married. We stood up for each other at our weddings. We went to high school together. He went on to University and a very successful business and executive career. I did other things.

When he and Marianne got married I was his best man. They took a driving trip for their honeymoon and wound up in New York City. At the time, I was working for a company based in New York City and offered to arrange some tickets for them for a play and a ballgame. One thing led to another and we wound up in New York at the same time.

We tried to stay out of their way, it being their honeymoon and all. Marianne claimed that it was great that we were in town because it gave them something interesting to do. At times like that I just duck.

New York City was New York City at that time. You could go anywhere. You could do anything. Even though Wanda was large with our first child and a heat wave had taken over the City, it was a great time. It was the first time in New York for any of us and it was everything we hoped it would be.

I had our New York office obtain tickets for the four of us to see My Fair Lady. I had also arranged for two tickets for Wanda and I to see the Roosevelt story, Sunrise at Campabello. When Wanda and I got to the box office at Sunrise at Campabello we discovered that the office had arranged and paid for four tickets to the play. Although it was right at show time, we knew our friends had gone to see a movie playing at a theatre in Times Square. I talked my way into three theatres and finally searched them out to deliver the news that we had the two additional Broadway tickets. It was quite an amazing feat, given the time and the crowds.

As a result, our first exposure to live theatre was at the very top. Live theatre has been a love of mine ever since, unlike Bridge where my first exposure to the game was terrible and I've hated it ever since.

We did all the tourist things. We rode the Circle Line Boat Tour around Manhattan. We went to the top of the Empire State Building. We saw the Yankees play Baltimore. We ate late with the "in" crowd. We heard the New York comedian say that "when he was a kid his father gave him a penny a day and a pat on the head. By the time he was twenty he had enough money for the down-payment on a house and a flat head." We thought it was funny. It was mind blowing being in the proverbial City that never sleeps.

It was all brand new and it took place in that space between the time that we were taking on the raising of families, big mortgages and difficult career choices and the time when we were really young kids.

My friend, the ultimate success, sat behind me in high school. We went to Cathedral High, which was a segregated boys only school taught, to a great degree, by priests. It was a tough school and the teachers, particularly the priests, had no difficulty in taking whatever disciplinary measures they felt were necessary.

It was the last period of the day and the teacher, Father D., had given us part of the period to use for study purposes or to get a jump on our homework. My friend Ted and I were using the time to exchange comments, chuckles and materials that we found amusing.

Father D., who had the reputation of being one of the mildest mannered priest/teachers in the school came along side us and quietly said to the both of us "you two boys stay after school for detention for an hour."

As my natural reaction to any penalty, deserved or not, was to register a protest I said-: "what for Father?"

I never even saw it coming. All of a sudden I found myself literally swatted out of my seat with a very sore side of my head and looked up to see the very mild mannered Father D. rubbing his very sore hand. It was indeed a display of "handing out" discipline.

My friend, the future CEO, Chairman, advisor to Premiers etc. had the opportunity of watching this entire scenario unfold in front of him. Much to my astonishment I sat there on the floor and heard my friend look at Father D. and say-: "yeah Father. What for?"

It was beautiful to watch. Another slow arching swing. A good connect to the side of the head. A second wise guy sitting on the floor wondering how it all happened.

Ted obviously got a lot smarter over the years. I'm not sure I ever did. All I know is that whenever I get the feeling that my friend is bigger than life I look back on the day when I watched a total disconnect between his eyes, his brain and his mouth. It was just another day at Cathedral High School.

The Prime Minister

In 1957 John Diefenbaker led the Conservative Party to a major landslide victory and became Prime Minister of Canada. Lester Pearson became the leader of the Liberal Party replacing Louis St. Laurent, who was long past his effective leadership days. The Liberals were suffering from terminal arrogance and made a number of mistakes that contributed to the Conservative win. Mr. Diefenbaker returned the favour by establishing his own style of arrogance and was defeated by Mr. Pearson in the next election. Mr. Pearson was in with a minority Government and shortly thereafter was forced into yet another election.

Pearson was a career diplomat and Nobel Peace Prize recipient who made the switch to the dog eat dog world of politics. Sometimes, he didn't seem to fit. He just came across as a very nice person and in many ways he just couldn't handle the pit bull style of Diefenbaker.

I started to get interested in politics around that time and volunteered to help out the local Liberal candidate. I was out there banging on doors and putting up signs and learning the grass roots part of politics. One thing led to another and I was asked to help look after the campaign in the Ancaster area. This usually means that the campaign is going very badly. Then one thing led to another and I was asked to look after the campaign for the entire district. This usually means that the campaign is going very, very badly. In other words, our guy was expected to lose and to lose big.

Being young and energetic, in other words stupid, I took on the job as campaign manager. The candidate and I got along very well. We tried some things that worked. Mr. Pearson turned out to be a more effective campaigner that many people expected and before we knew it, we were suddenly back in the race.

As the campaign was winding down, the people running the national campaign for Mr. Pearson scheduled him to come into Hamilton for a major speech and rally. He was to travel by car from Kitchener on a Tuesday afternoon. At that time the most direct route from Kitchener to Hamilton was through the town of Dundas. Our candidate had his headquarters right on the main street of Dundas and Mr. Pearson would pass right by our front door.

I was immediately onto the national campaign people with the request that Mr. Pearson stop by our headquarters and give us a great photo opportunity.

I was told, in no uncertain terms, that our guy was a loser and that Mr. Pearson would not be stopping by. The decision was protested by me in the form of new poll results that showed we were in a race, by calls from every Liberal of influence that I could find and by personal pleading. I made the point that they were definitely relegating us to a loser role if he just drove on past without stopping and as Mr. Pearson was also in a close race, this would be unwise.

Finally, they relented and agreed to stop for a fifteen minute visit, provided I could guarantee that the headquarters would be filled with people as they did not want Mr. Pearson coming into a semi-empty hall. I, of course, agreed that would pose no problem. I assured them the place would be jammed and people would be spilling out onto the sidewalk. The deal was made.

There is a great scene in the old movie "The Quiet Man". The Protestant Bishop is to visit the local Protestant Minister. As the town is almost totally Catholic, the Minister has almost no congregation and, as a result may be moved away, but he is loved and admired by everyone in town. The townspeople who want to do everything they can to prevent his transfer decide that they will line the roadway and greet the Bishop as he arrives in town by carriage accompanied by the Minister.

Even the old Catholic priest gets involved and forms part of the crowd lining the road. As the carriage approaches the priest hides his Roman collar with a kerchief and instructs his congregation with the words, "Now when they arrive in front of you I want you all to cheer like Protestants."

The instant crowd worked in the movies so I thought we could probably make it work in real life as well. If you have ever been asked to mobilize a crowd on a Tuesday afternoon you would be well advised to decline the honour. I called everyone I knew or knew of. I chased Liberals, Conservatives, Socialists, relatives, neighbours, acquaintances and a few people that were just in the area. Finally, I felt confident that I had enough people committed to the endeavour that we could fill the hall on a Tuesday afternoon. Everything was confirmed with the national campaign team and we awaited the big day.

A week before the scheduled visit we received a call from the Mayor of Dundas.

"I understand you people have arranged to have the Prime Minister visit Dundas."

"We have indeed, Mr. Mayor," I replied.

"Well I'm not too happy about him coming into town without stopping by City Hall and signing our VIP guest book. I hope you can get him to do that because I'm not sure who I'll endorse in this next election but, remember, I've got some political clout."

"I'll see what I can do, Mr. Mayor but it will be a battle because I know he's on a tight schedule and they want to get him into Hamilton so that he can get some rest before the speech and rally."

I was after the national campaign people again and explained the circumstances and assured them that the Town Hall was only a block and a half away from our headquarters so the Prime Minister could do both visits. I even suggested that, as the two sites were so close, Mr. Pearson could walk from one to the other and do some "main streeting" as the common man. They agreed, reluctantly, but with the proviso that there would be a significant crowd at the Town Hall when the Prime Minister arrived.

I said, "no problem."

The big day arrived and, as promised, the headquarters was jammed with people. My nephew Jim had his little girl there to present a bouquet of flowers to Mrs. Pearson. There was much cheering, photo taking, hand shaking and congratulations all around. We then set out for our walk to the Town Hall. I accompanied Mr. & Mrs. Pearson, along with the candidate, and had arranged to have a couple of people stop the Prime Minister and ask him a question or just shake his hand. This was before the days of top security, terrorists and the like, so a minor delay was not a problem. I needed the time because I had another game, literally, afoot.

The alleyway behind our headquarters opened up onto the street just in front of the old Town Hall. I had organized my campaign helpers to hustle the headquarters crowd out the back door, hustle them down the alleyway and form them up again on and around the steps at the Town Hall. It worked. There was more than a little huffing and puffing in evidence but there they stood, all smiles, waiting for the Prime Minister.

The Mayor of Dundas stood on the steps decked out in his chain of office, all abeam. He may have even thought this sudden surge of humanity was there to see him.

I walked proudly up the steps with Mr. Pearson and our local candidate. We all shook hands with the Mayor and other Council members that had shown up. Mr. Pearson shook hands with people in the crowd and as we were being ushered into the Town Hall so the book could be signed, Mr. Pearson leaned over to me with a big grin and said, "You know son, I think I've seen some of these people before."

"I wouldn't be surprised, Mr. Prime Minister. You have a great reputation for never forgetting a face."

Our candidate won in an upset. Mr. Pearson won a close election. It was a good day. I was never sure who the Mayor of Dundas voted for that year but he seemed to like Mr. Pearson.

Bonds for Israel

My Dad was Irish and my mother was German. I've often thought how much more difficult life would have been had I genetically received the German sense of humour and the Irish sense of order instead of the other way around.

My mother was Lutheran and my father was Roman Catholic. I was raised a Catholic. I attended St. Ann's School at Sherman and Barton streets while all my pals attended Adelaide Hoodless School on Springer Avenue. When it came time to join the Boy Scouts my father sent me off to Ryerson United because that's where my friends were going. Forget all about the scout troops at St. Patricks or at Holy Family. "Learn with and learn from your friends", was preached by my father.

One of the fondest thoughts I have of my father is that he did not seem to harbour a single bigoted thought or have a bigoted bone in his body. I had no idea that there was any difference between any race, colour or creed. I got that from my father and try to pass it along as best as I can. We, too, often, run into a different attitude. As Rogers and Hammerstein laid out in a great song about prejudice from the play South Pacific, "You've Got to be Taught" when it comes to those types of things.

My father loved the Brooklyn Dodgers. Fortunately for him, he died before the Dodgers moved away from Brooklyn to Los Angeles, acquired fancy Hollywood friends and went up scale. I've never forgiven them either and I've left my Brooklyn Dodger hat with my daughter Linda as a major part of my estate.

He particularly got himself worked up when the Dodgers were playing the hated New York Yankees. As a little guy, I asked him why. He told me he usually liked to cheer for the underdog.

"What's an underdog?" I wanted to know.

He explained that an underdog was the person, side or group that wasn't expected to win. He explained that all too often people jump on the bandwagon that cheers for the obvious winner. That made sense to me. The bandwagon for the favourite is too often too crowded to be comfortable anyway.

No one had to teach me about the horrors of World War II and about the even greater horrors that resulted from the need of one race to totally subjugate another. No one had to teach me about the horrors that come from the need of one race to annihilate another. That came very naturally to me. It has been reinforced by events from time to time.

I've always admired President Harry Truman. I particularly admired his courage and that of those around him in working to establish the State of Israel. Israel was established, and despite occasional errors in judgement, in my mind the State of Israel deserves to be there and deserves help when needed in order to assure survival.

In my mind, the "War" is World War II. There is also Korea, Vietnam, the Gulf, Afghanistan etc. They are all known by their own names and as war is such a part of our lives it's easier to keep track if you put a proper name to the event. As turmoil in the Middle East in and around Israel has been around since time began and history has been recorded, it's hard to put individual names on the wars that took place in the region. Because of this, I'm unable to recall which war it was but it was clearly a war that Israel was about to lose. This means, of course, that if you lose just once you will probably disappear forever.

Watching events unfold with this particular conflict and being convinced that Israel was about to lose, I called my friend Larry and asked him how I would go about buying some Bonds for Israel. Larry knows about such things.

He advised me that it was clearly a bad investment and asked why I wanted to do such a thing, especially in that Israel looked like it would be gone. I agreed with his assessment on both counts. I explained that I wanted to buy the bonds with one in the name of each of my children who were quite young at the time.

Larry asked me why I would do that and I explained that if our assessments were correct and if Israel lost and, indeed, did disappear I wanted my children to one day look at the Bonds and wonder why their father would have done such a thing. That way they might have a better understanding of why their old man felt the way he did about such things as underdogs, prejudice, Harry Truman and, in a small way, Beau Geste.

Larry will have probably forgotten the incident. The transaction was small and he has always had so much going on in his life and in his head that I wouldn't expect him to remember the request. We were always very good friends and remain so to this day. I like to think that even if he doesn't remember the incident it helped fuel a friendship that spans decades.

Many years later the banks in their wisdom closed out my construction business the week before Christmas. I saw it coming. I battled for two years against ever increasing interest rates and an ever shrinking construction market. The bank finally got me.

I lost the business I had worked with for twenty-five years. I lost my life savings. I lost my home and my farm. I had no mental, physical or financial resources left. I was totally worn out emotionally. I felt I had let every one down, including my family. I was devastated.

I had the support of my wife and my family but it was an awful time. I was particularly beaten down by the incident where a bank representative had come to our house on a Sunday afternoon when Wanda and I were at work and talked his way into our home past our teenaged daughter so that he could make an assessment of the property values for his employers.

There was such a need to talk to somebody. I called and arranged a meeting with my old friend Larry at his office. He listened to my story of how everything was gone. He listened to me tell him of how totally beaten up I felt after two years of battling the inevitable. He watched me put my face in my hands and heard me cry.

After a bit and when I had pulled myself somewhat back together, Larry quietly said to me:

"Is that all? You've lost your business and where you live? Is that all?" "I thought it was something real serious. Something you couldn't handle. Something like a death in the family or someone close had a terminal disease", he said.

Perspective. What a speech. What a sermon. What a homily. What beautiful timing.

I hope Larry remembers the incident. I hope, if he doesn't, someone reminds him of it. I've tried to remind him of it occasionally but he sloughs it off. Both Larry and Marnie just go through life doing nice things and being great people. God, old friends are great.

I Really Need a Loan

I feel sad for those persons who can't allow others to enjoy Christmas.

We live in a world where we drive down the streets and highways shaking our fists at each other. We give each other the finger. We refuse to let anyone merge onto our road. We slam doors in each other's faces. We bump into people, then curse at them because they weren't watching where they were going. We seem to now take this as acceptable behaviour.

Then Christmas rolls around and we put up with people telling us how awful it is to wish or be wished a Merry Christmas. How bad can that be?

This is not a rant about exclusion or inclusion. This is just a comment on priorities that seem to be badly mixed up. It has nothing to do with faith or religion. It's about people and our difficulty in not letting some enjoyment spill out now and again.

We usually spend Christmas Eve visiting good friends and sharing stories. We understand that by Christmas Eve any thought of food restraint has been put aside. We know there are several boxes of chocolates and cookies that need to be cleaned up so that the diet can re-commence. We don't drink and drive. I try to listen to a little of the Paul Reid Christmas program on the radio. It's a program about memories and nice things. We contemplate the enjoyment that our friends and loved ones may take from their gifts. It is not about faith but, sometimes, the good feelings that come from it restores some of our faith in people.

Christmas, like most festivals, is very much about kids. Perhaps there are some kids in the world that have been damaged by believing, for a while, in Santa Claus or the Easter Bunny or in Jack and the Beanstock. I haven't met them. On the other hand, I have met a number of adults that have led badly skewed lives because they have gone through life believing in Santa Claus.

One Christmas Eve, we were sitting in the living room with some friends. There were a number of very young children in the room whose attention would be grabbed by the radio announcer who was issuing half hour reports on the progress of Santa Claus. He would announce that an unidentified flying object was reported on radar heading south from the North Pole. This caused some tension.

Next we would hear that the UFO had been identified as a sleigh being pulled by eight animals. More tension and a four year old announced, "see I told you."

A short while later the announcer told us that the sleigh was identified as carrying Santa Claus and that it was now approaching North Bay. The announcer suggested that children had better be getting ready for bed. The next announcement, preceded by the sound of jingling bells, informed us that the sleigh had now left North Bay and was believed to be heading in our direction. The announcer, with some urgency in his voice, now stated that all children who expected Santa Claus to call should be on their way to bed.

A five year old little guy at our gathering ran and looked out the window, hoping I'm sure, to see a mysterious object in the sky. Instead, he saw an older boy strolling nonchalantly down the street with a hockey stick over his shoulder.

Absolutely certain that the kid on the street was about to blow the Santa visit for everyone, he grabbed his father by the sleeve, dragged him to the window and implored,

"Get that kid off the street."

Several years later we met the five year old again. He seemed fairly well adjusted. In fact, he had made himself quite a successful career as a banker. His main complaint was that too many people were looking for ill advised loans from his bank.

"They must think I'm Santa Claus" he complained.

There are times that loans make sense. There are times they are desperately needed. Sometimes, that happens in and around Christmas.

Donna and Dale each brought two children into their second marriage. They are the types of people that immediately made all the children their children. The children are all close in age but Tom, the only boy, has to contend with three sisters. That can be tough.

I don't know Tom well but I can sympathize with his position as the only boy in a family of four and I can understand some of his thought process. Apparently, one Christmas Tom decided that he had found the ideal gift for his entire family. His school was selling giant sized chocolate bars as a fund raiser. Tom had his Christmas shopping money ready and purchased four of the bars. Donna and the three sisters were covered. Dale was let in on the deal.

The chocolate bars were secreted into his room, carefully wrapped and hidden away for the big day. It's said that timing is everything in life. Unfortunately, Tom's timing was off just a little bit.

The day before Christmas, Tom approached his father and announced that he had a problem. He needed to arrange a loan.

"What for?" Dale asked.

"I need to do my Christmas shopping and I don't have any money," explained Tom.

"You told me you got your Christmas shopping done".

"Well, I kinda don't have the presents anymore," said Tom.

"You mean to tell me, that over the past two weeks you wrapped then unwrapped and ate four giant chocolate bars"?

"I guess that's what happened," answered Tom.

He got his loan. I never did find out what he gave Donna and his sisters for Christmas. It doesn't matter. It's one of those stories that gets told around the family table. It's one of the memories.

Someone just wanted to do something nice for his family and that should be just fine by everyone. Believe me, it's not about religion.

Pipe Cleaning

When we were first married, Wanda and I lived in an apartment in my mother's house on Prospect Street. It was cheap and it was convenient when it came to helping out my mother.

After a short while we moved to an apartment on the next street over for reasons that all kinds of people who have lived with a parent or in-law could understand.

I was sitting in the bath tub one Saturday morning when the door burst open and Wanda hurried into the bathroom and proceeded to retch into the toilet. Now, Wanda at that point in her life was a very quiet young lady that was almost always on her very best behaviour.

When I heard her come up from her retching and saw her look me straight in the eye and say, "You #%$&#@%, I knew I was going to be a father.

We were nice and snug in our little home. We had enough money to pay the rent and buy groceries. We even had enough left over to buy tobacco products. We would re-work the budget every time I got a five dollar raise and, by being careful, we could occasionally come up with enough money and gasoline to drive out to Barb and Ed's Hotdog Stand for a really nice evening out.

I smoked a pipe at the time. It gave me a debonair, worldly look that I knew would stand me in good stead as a young man making his way in the world and as a young father. Second hand smoke was unheard of in those days.

Somewhere I had managed to acquire a Sherlock Holmes style curved pipe. It was great for effect and even produced a good smoke but the crooked stem was notorious for collecting flungdungen that was produced from the juices and waste in the tobacco. As we had more than a little time on our hands I had become quite adept at pipe cleaning.

This was done using a cotton covered flexible wire that was used to push the aforementioned flungdungen out of the pipe and on to a tissue.

It worked very well on all my pipes except for the Sherlock Holmes pipe. The little reservoir in the pipe stem kept jamming up and I couldn't push the wire through from either end.

I had previously established to Wanda and myself that I was not the brightest pipe cleaner person in the world. In order to speed up the cleaning process of my pipes I had once taken several of them, threw them into a pot of boiling water that also had a spoonful of honey in the mix for "mellowness" and left them on the boil for several minutes. The resultant damage to the pipes, mess in the pot and foul odour from the boiling had a direct bearing on our decision to move out of our apartment in my mother's house.

However, getting back to my Sherlock Holmes pipe cleaning adventure, I had been cleaning a number of other pipes that evening and had built up a supply of dirty tissues in an ashtray that was situated on a small table between my chair and the sheer curtains. The cleaning of the Sherlock Holmes pipe had come to a standstill because of the flungdungen that was trapped in the middle of the pipe stem.

Being the clever devil that I am, I figured that if I poured lighter fluid into each end of the pipe and lit it on fire, the flame would eat its way to the middle of the pipe and like magic the obstruction would be destroyed. I could detect no flaw in the plan and proceeded.

I carefully filled each end of the pipe stem, which included filling the pipe bowl itself. I took a firm grip on the centre of the pipe stem and lit it up.

Fire blew out from both ends. I mean it blew out from both ends. It took approximately ten seconds for the entire pipe to heat up to the point where I could no longer hold onto it. What do you do under those circumstances?

I dropped it into the ashtray that, of course, already held a mixture of about eight torn tissues from my earlier pipe cleaning endeavours. Up they went. The sheer curtains were within reach and they were next.

I was now beating out tissues and trying to smother a pipe that had gone berserk while holding the sheer curtains away from the inferno and yelling for water.

Wanda looked in and saw what was happening. A pot of water brought it under control and kept us from moving again so quickly. When it was all over the quiet sweet Wanda for the second time in a very short while looked me in the eye and said, "You really are a dumb #%@&%#."

Moose Hunting

I do not intend to seek a fight with hunters. First of all they have guns. Secondly, they are much better organized than I will ever be and thirdly, I eat beef, pork, chicken and a bunch of other things that I have people kill on my behalf.

As I said, I don't intend to seek a fight with hunters. I just don't want to be one.

As a very young teen-ager I recall getting up real early when I was camping and quietly walking along a ridge with no one else around. The land was fairly heavily forested and dropped off rather steeply to a small creek that ran through the area. I heard a sound that was almost a rustling noise accompanied by an occasional sound of twigs or sticks snapping. I sat down and watched the area below me as the sound was moving in my direction.

The most beautiful buck, sporting a set of six or eight point antlers, was running alongside the creek. It was really more a graceful lope than a run. It just effortlessly cleared dead fallen trees and moved with a grace that was absolutely breath taking. It never knew I was there. It never knew it was being watched. It just ran for the sake of running. I watched it until it disappeared. It ended any chance that I could ever be a hunter.

Over several years I had the opportunity of flying into lakes in northern Quebec to do some fishing. I know that it's rationalizing, to a degree, but I'm okay with fishing. Perhaps it's because you usually have the option of releasing a fish but you have no such option once you've let fly at an animal with a chunk of lead. We had some great fishing trips with various mixes of fishermen. Twice, I had the pleasure of taking such a trip with my son Dan.

On one of the trips a friend of mine and myself were trolling very quietly and following a shore line towards the mouth of a small bay. Fishing can be a very quiet way to enjoy a piece of life. Some of the greatest conversations I have ever had have been with a fellow fisherman in a boat where neither person talks. It tells you a lot about people. This was one of those times.

As we rounded the shore line into the opening to the bay we spotted two moving things in the water. We stayed well back but recognized a mother moose and a very young calf swimming across the entrance to the bay. It was a swim of almost a hundred yards.

The little guy had put his trust in Mom and was doggedly keeping up with her as she worked her way. The banks were rocky and fairly steep. When they got to the far bank, the little guy was obviously out of gas. The swim had taken every bit of energy he had, to the point where he couldn't make his way out of the water and up the bank.

Mom moved behind him and used her forehead and strength to boost the calf out of the water and up onto dry ground. The little guy just laid straight out. Roy and I fished the bay for about an hour. We trolled past the place where the calf was stretched out stacking zeds under the protection of Mom. The adult moose stood so perfectly still over him that, had we not witnessed her actions, we would never have known she was standing watch. On one of our trips around we saw that, nap over, they had disappeared into the bush. Perhaps they should have been shot or otherwise harvested but, somehow, it seemed real good to know that they were out there.

We once saw Hal Holbrook do his reading impressions of Mark Twain. The satire and the humour of Twain is a joy. The bite of some of his comment is classic and a reminder that we should never lose sight of social conscience. Some of his stuff is so poignant that laughter can be turned to tears very quickly. Holbrook did Twain beautifully.

He was especially effective to me when he recited a piece that Twain had written describing the look of the Mississippi through the eyes of a riverboat pilot. Twain described the motion of the boat, the movement of the river, the passing of the trees that were partially hidden by the early morning mists. His ambition in life had been to become a riverboat pilot and he made it. Unfortunately, right at that time the American Civil War, the railroads and the move to the west was bringing river commerce to an end and Twain knew it. If you ever have the need to describe poignancy you should go to this particular reading.

Dan and I had a morning much like the one described by Twain. We were alone and were quietly working our way into a shallow bay very early in the morning. Twain's motion of the boat, his movement of the water, the rising mists were all there that morning.

As we drifted into the bay we saw a full grown moose standing "armpit" deep in the water and feeding on the tender underwater shoots along the edge of the bay. A moose is an ugly animal. It's also a very dangerous animal if it feels threatened. We gave the moose a wide berth but enjoyed the watch. The moose paid almost no attention to us and behaved in a manner that suggested no fear of these strange creatures that were intruding on a tranquil feeding scene.

It made me mad.

I thought, it won't be long before creatures such as us will be sliding up as closely as possible to such an animal and then taking their thundersticks and blowing a hole into it. They would then take each others picture with their trophy and butcher out a few choice roasts to take home and impress their friends.

Dan and I decided to scream and yell at the animal. We decided to throw a couple of the things we had in the boat at it. We wanted to scare the animal and we did. We wanted it to know that creatures in a boat are a threat. The moose bolted and we were pleased.

As I said earlier, I don't really have anything against hunters. I just don't want to be one.

Stranger on the Shore

I met Alan through business. Wanda and I met Margaret a short time later. We started as a business connection and we have remained good friends ever since. We saw each others kids grow up. We attended at their weddings.

Margaret and Alan are British by birth and, in many ways, remain British by attitude. They have also become very Canadian but, thank goodness, they have retained much of the "get on with it" attitude that has served Britain so well.

We were especially impressed when we decided to visit Stratford together to take in a play and increase our cultural quotient. Margaret instructed us to put aside any concerns we might have about lunch and to let her provide a proper British picnic instead. We set out our blanket on the banks of the Avon River and whiled away a good part of the afternoon, sipping on a fine wine, watching the swans and the peddle boats and sampling British style sandwiches and cookies. It was great.

Alan and Margaret had met, wooed and wed in Britain. They observed that they often spent time beside a little lake listening to the tunes of a very popular British musician and band leader by the name of Acker Bilk. The favourite Acker Bilk song was called "Stranger on the Shore". The scene and the grounds at Stratford reminded them of the courting days listening to Acker Bilk.

We see each other several times each year and make a point of not losing touch. When too much time has passed between touches, one or the other of us recognizes that fact and we get it fixed. The result has been some great meals at each other's homes, some great times out, an occasional short excursion and some good concerts.

When I found that Acker Bilk was touring Canada and had Hamilton as a stop, I immediately arranged four tickets as I knew this would be a "can't miss" event for Alan and Margaret. They were delighted that I had obtained tickets and we put together an evening that included dinner out at a local steakhouse, the concert and then drinks in the Hamilton Place lounge after the show. The visit to the lounge was of special interest because Acker Bilk, himself, was expected to stop by after the show and spend some additional time with his fans.

As we were coming from different directions we agreed to meet at the steakhouse, have dinner, leave one car parked at the restaurant and ride to Hamilton Place together. We had a delightful but typical steakhouse dinner. We enjoyed the garlic bread, a Caesar Salad and a fine steak with a butter style light gravy highlighting the steak. A pre-dinner drink and a bottle of wine sent us off to the concert in a nice mellow mood.

The mood was somewhat challenged when Alan and Margaret got into the back seat of our car to drive to the concert hall. Wanda, earlier that day, had picked up some Pampas Grass plants to use as decorations. Pampas Grass grows tall and has feathery type plumes that gives them a special style and makes them attractive decorations. They are also very messy and shed their feathers indiscriminately.

As Wanda had placed the plants in the back seat of the car and as the plants had done a little shedding before she got them home, there were a few "feathers" scattered on the back seat.

When Alan and Margaret got into the car and I was asked whether we had been keeping chickens in the back, it did test the mellowness just a little. Nevertheless, we knew Acker Bilk would make everything okay.

It was a great concert. It was especially appreciated by people who knew the musician from their British homeland. It brought back a lot of memories for them.

Following the concert we quickly made our way into the lounge and made certain we had a prominent table, just in case Acker Bilk did show up and proved to be approachable. There he was at the very next table.

Margaret, losing most of her normal British reserve, moved on the poor man like a schoolgirl at a Frank Sinatra concert. A little talking, a sharing of stories about places they both knew in Britain, some reminiscences about when and where "Stranger on the Shore" was first heard and then a dance or two. What an evening.

All good things come to an end and an evening that started with Garlic Bread and Caesar Salad ended with Margaret finishing a dance with her young lass entertainment idol. Margaret asked him for a goodnight kiss. Acker Bilk happily obliged.

As she was floating away from the encounter she was brought suddenly back to earth when she heard her dancing partner call her name.

"Margaret" he called.

"Yes Acker" she replied.

"I love the garlic," said Acker with a smile.

Crash!

At least I didn't hear a lot of nonsense and complaining about how I should be embarrassed over keeping chickens in the back seat of the car.

Mont Tremblant

Herman Schmidt, my ski instructor from Hotel Suisse, had given up on me by the time we were taken to Mont Tremblant as part of our ski resort package. Tremblant had the highest ski runs and the most ski runs in Eastern Canada. The excursion also provided us with our first experience with a major chair lift operation.

In preparation for using the chair lift we were given a number of instructions. We were told to shuffle into the tracks in front of the chair. The workmen would hold the chair for a brief moment as you sat down. They would then release the chair and flip the safety bar over your head so that it would rest in front of you on your lap. You would then lock it down. Wanda was in line immediately in front of me. She was brave but was obviously very concerned over the ride she was about to take and about the vehicle that would take her on the ride. Her concern increased as she watched the workmen casually flip safety bars so hard that they often bounced backwards or so easy that they never came over your head. As the chair was constantly moving, the skier would be required to reach behind, grab the safety bar and lift it back into place before the chair reached an altitude that could be as much as sixty feet in the air. It was actually quite a dangerous manoeuvre.

All the workmen spoke only French. Wanda didn't. I watched as she took her position in front of the chair and as she instructed the workmen, in no uncertain terms, on what she expected of them. Even though she wore ski mitts I could see finger pointing and finger waggling. Even though she was instructing French speaking people in English, she was making herself very clearly understood. The workmen would dig in their heels, grab the chair and hold on with all their strength, see that she was safely seated, then gently lift the safety bar over her head and send her on her way. A smile and a "merci" and she was up the hill. After watching that episode I've always refused to believe that people cannot be made to understand each other and, if expressed correctly, there is no language barrier.

It was a beautiful day for skiing. It was cold but not blowing. The sun was shining on the lower runs but it was snowing very gently at the top of the mountain. We had been told that it was the fiftieth consecutive day they had snowfalls at the top of Tremblant. Riding the chair lift allowed you to see for miles.

We found a run that stretched for almost three miles. You could ski it hard by going straight down the fall line, or you could swing back and forth across the trail and enjoy a much more gentle decent. For the most part, we did the latter.

My friend Russ and I were taking a rest and standing by the side of the trail when we noticed a rather unusual skier further up the hill. He was unusual in that he was wearing a form of overcoat, baggy work style pants and a large woolen toque pulled over his ears. The style of the day was that everything fit tight. He was also covered in snow from head to foot.

We watched as he would ski for ten or fifteen yards then fold up and collapse in a heap. He would then struggle to his feet, brush off some snow and repeat the process. It was like watching an accident unfold in slow motion steps. It was a painful way to make progress but he gradually worked his way downhill towards where we were standing.

Finally he reached where we were standing and watching. By reaching where we were standing, I mean he crashed at our feet in another heap of flying snow. He got back up on his skis, brushed himself off, removed a mitt and stuck his hand out to us.

"Excuse me, gentlemen", he said in a broad English accent that would make Prince Charles proud, "I realize we have not been formally introduced but could either of you chaps explain to me how one stops on these damn things?"

It's so nice to observe the proprieties, isn't it?

It was a great day of skiing. As it wound down another of our friends told us of a trail that came down from the very top of the mountain. If you ski it a certain way, even relative novices like us could pick our way down safely and avoid serious drops. We convinced our wives to give it a try along with us.

Fifty consecutive days of snowfall had really produced a wonderland. The snow was hard, cold blue. Simon and Garfunkel were right. You could hear the sound of silence. We picked our way along the trail and when we spoke to each other it was kind of hushed. No one wanted to disturb the moment. It was worth every cold morning drive, every bruise, every scrape and every aching muscle it took to be able to ski just well enough to go there and feel it. It was great.

We did some skiing after we got home from our trip. Wanda broke her leg on a silly little hill in Orangeville. I watched her hobble around and go through all the required therapy to get over the break and decided to give up the sport. While she was recovering from the injury we took another driving holiday through Pennsylvania. It was springtime. The flowers were just coming into bloom. The Catfish were jumping in the Susquehanna River. The birds were singing in the trees. Nine months later we had Linda.

Cattle Auction

Never name a cow that you intend to eat. Actually, people don't really eat cows all that often. They eat beef cattle but the principal is the same.

My friend Russ and I once bought a piece of scrub farmland as a speculative investment. I can't remember why we selected the area we chose other than that the land was cheap and part of the property was fenced. It also had a very old house that we could rent out to help defray some costs. As part of the property was fenced, we were successful in renting some of the land to a local farmer who wanted some extra space to graze some of his cattle.

A condition of our rental arrangement included the right to buy a steer ourselves and turn it out to pasture with the farmer's cattle for grazing.

Neither Russ nor I knew the first thing about buying cattle. We didn't even know where or how such things even took place. Our farmer friend directed us to the Ancaster Auction Barns and we were told that the beef cattle were brought in for auction sale on Thursday afternoons. The following Thursday, we were there all primed and ready to become cattlemen. We were slightly over-dressed for the occasion. We left our jackets in the car and we even had gone so far as to loosen our ties. Somehow, we still stuck out a little from the blue jeaned or cover-alled farmers that were there to buy or sell.

I was a little leery about animal auctions. I knew it was an "as is" final sale so it was very much a buyer beware situation. Someone once told me about a horse auction where a rather shaggy and ungroomed mare was brought into the ring for sale.

"She doesn't look so good", said the auctioneer, "but she's gentle and she's an easy keeper."

The mare was sold and as she was being walked out of the ring by her new owner, she walked straight into a post.

"The horse is blind," complained the new owner.

"That's what I told you," answered the auctioneer. "She doesn't look so good."

Russ and I settled on our benches determined not to be out-hustled by a bunch of farmers. We decided to watch a few animals go through the sale and get a fix on both quality and price. We noted that bid prices usually jumped in increments of two to five cents per pound. Occasionally, prices would move at ten cents per pound in the early bidding for a particularly good looking animal. Bidders would indicate their bid by a small motion of the hand that would be acknowledged by the auctioneer calling out the new bid price.

Russ and I sat side by side watching and learning. Finally, out trotted a great looking Hereford cross heifer.

"This is a buy. Let's not miss this one", said Russ.

I can't recall the prices but it seems to me that beef cattle was selling at an average of $1.30 per pound, on the hoof, at that time.

The bidding opened at eighty cents. I indicated a bid of ninety cents. It moved to a dollar and I indicated $1.10. It jumped to $1.20 and I motioned $1.30. A $1.40 was bid but I wasn't about to be scared off and the auctioneer accepted my bid of $1.50. The price immediately went to $1.60 and even though I was now starting to panic, I said $1.70.

The auctioneer and a growing number of farmers seemed to be taking some extra delight in my refusal to back off the deal. The bid went to $1.80. I took it to $1.85. The auctioneer, now grinning ear to ear, looked at Russ and I and asked, "Is there any chance you two city fellas are together?"

We allowed as how we were.

"Maybe", he suggested, you outta not be bidding against each other on the same animal. Just a suggestion, fellas."

It seems that ever since my bid of $1.10, which I indicated by moving my right hand, Russ was raising in ten cent increments by moving his left hand. Thank God the auctioneer took mercy on us or we might still be there.

It cost us another fee to move the animal to our property up in Haldimand County. Russ named the animal Hortense for no particular reason, but it meant that neither of us could now have her killed because we knew her name.

We sold the farm two years later. It was a 100 acre property and we probably made $2,000 on the deal. Hortense was sold with the farm. She was fat and happy the last time we saw her.

By the way, a year later Stelco and Ontario Hydro paid someone huge bucks to buy all the farms in that immediate area. It wasn't us.

Looking for Contractors

The Jesuit order of priests have often been a bane to the Catholic Church and, specifically, to various Popes. The Jesuits have been able to attract some very clever persons who heard a calling to the religious life that was sometimes different from others who became priests. Their positions taken on liturgical matters have left them at sixes and sevens with the mainstream of the Church on many occasions.

My limited experience and contact with the Jesuits left me with considerable admiration for their preaching abilities, their expressed sense of logic and their independence within an organization that does not reward independence. I don't believe you will ever see a Jesuit elected Pope.

When we were in the pile driving business, we bid on a job for a Jesuit seminary that was to be built. We bid as a sub contractor to a general contractor that was to control and coordinate the work. We discovered that our company was the low bidder for our portion of the project and we were expecting to receive a contract at any time.

Instead of receiving the expected contract, we received a telephone call from Father M. who, at that time was the head person of the Jesuit order in the area. We had previously learned that Father M. had taken a great interest in the design of the building and that he held degrees both as a Lawyer and as a Civil Engineer.

Father M. introduced himself and explained that the project was significantly over budget and that he, as a result, had taken over the buying of the sub contractors from the general contractor. This was highly unusual but Father M. made it clear that he was taking over the job and that he intended to save some money and get the project done on budget.

I was brought into what had become a conference call with my partner, Father M. and myself. It went something like this-:

Father M.- "I'm buying the sub contractor work because we need to save some money and get this project done within budget."

My Partner- "let's see if we can help."

Father M.- "Hope so. This is what I've done so far. I realize you had the lowest bid but I spoke with your main competitor and he managed to save some money and his bid is now about $10,000 lower than yours. Do you want to do anything about it?"

We agreed that we would take a look at our estimate and get back to him.

My partner and I went over our costs. We decided we could save some money by re-approaching some of our suppliers and by removing some contingency items we had in the bid. After about three hours work, we called Father M. back.

"Father, we've gone over things and we can drop our estimate by approximately $15,000 which leaves us back as low bidder."

"I'll get back to you," promised Father M.

Two days later we received another call from the good Father.

"Fellows," he said, "I've talked to your competitors again and they decided they could change some things and dropped their price by another $10,000. That leaves them lower than you. Do you want to take another look at your figures?"

Somewhat annoyed, we agreed that we would.

The next day we called him back and told him that by increasing our estimated production slightly and by removing the weather contingency and by lowering our profit margin significantly, we could reduce our price by another $10,000 and leave us as low bidder. He promised he would get back to us shortly and thanked us for helping him out.

We got the call.

"Fellows, I spoke with your competitors again and, much to my surprise they lowered their price and they are slightly under you again. Do you want to do anything about it," he asked.

My partner was really upset at the way this whole thing was being handled and said,

"Father, we've done everything we can reasonably do to help you out with this project. I'm really disappointed with how this has been handled. I'm especially surprised, as a good Catholic, that a person in your position would turn this whole process into an auction. It's just not the way I would expect it to be handled."

There was a pause then Father M. came back.

"I'm not looking for good Catholics today, Joe. I'm looking for good contractors. Are you interested or not?"

We didn't get the job. I'm sure, however, that it was built on budget. I can understand how the Pope sometimes has problems with those guys.

Score Keeping

I really had a passion for baseball as a kid and as a young adult.

I don't think much of the game now filled with wandering free agents and even wandering franchises. If you want to know the starting line-up of the 1948 Cleveland Indians, I'm your man. I can even give you the starting line-up of the 1948 Hamilton Cardinals.

Please, just don't ask me what I had for dinner yesterday or what my wife was wearing when she went out for groceries. I just can't remember.

My Dad died when I was fourteen. He took me out for a drive when I was twelve and he explained about a biopsy and cancer and a bunch of things I really wasn't ready to learn. He took the next two years to die and I took the next two years to grow from the age of twelve to about the age of thirty.

One of the very few things, perhaps the only thing, that's might be considered good about cancer is that it sometimes gives the victim the opportunity to do some things that might otherwise get overlooked or postponed.

My Dad was a baseball fan. I mean, he was a really big baseball fan. He is the only person I know that would argue an umpire's call when he was listening to a game on the radio. Thank God we never had television at that point in our lives. Any baseball game was worth watching as far as he was concerned.

He would stop and watch a sandlot softball game. He would watch school games. He had never seen a major league game but checked the standings every morning and read the line scores in the paper. The tone of the morning could well be set by the prowess of the Brooklyn Dodgers the day before.

He and I went to the Hamilton Cardinals, Class D, games whenever we could. The ballpark was just down the street and the admission was cheap. I like to believe that he took me with him because he knew how much I loved the game but I know that part of the reason was that his illness would sometimes cause him to pass out without warning. I guess I was a little bit of his security blanket but for me, it was a great evening out with my Dad.

Somewhere along the way I had learned how to score a baseball game. Programs cost about five cents and I had it figured out that I could buy a score book for a quarter that had fifty pages in it. I would carry my score book when we went to the games and would list the batting orders and keep the account of the game. I thought it was neat. My father, at first, wanted none of it.

"What's the point of all that?" he asked.

"It lets me mark down everything that happens. Then, if I want I can check back on every situation during the game. If I feel like it I can replay the game in my head when I get home."

"That's a lot of nonsense. It just distracts you from watching the game".

"No it doesn't. It makes me pay even better attention" I replied as I went about my business of marking singles, double plays, strike outs and fly balls to centre.

Usually after the first couple of innings he would lean over when I was marking something and he'd say, "What's that mean?"

"That shows that the batter singled but the runner was thrown out going from first to third."

"What would you have marked down if he had scored and the batter went to second?"

I would show him. Before long the score card and pencil would be in his hand. The questions would come and the markings in my score book would become his. After the first two such episodes the score book became his and I was relegated to the role of consultant. He took the book to every game we attended. Sometimes we would need to leave early because of his sickness and I would carry the book home. I would have an arm around me and felt good because there was the touch between father and son but knew, in my heart, that there was a little leaning going on because he was in difficulty.

I never went to another major league game after the strike that cancelled the World Series. I had taken in as many games as I could up to that time. A good friend of mine arranged to have us take in a game in a fancy corporate box at the Sky Dome. I remember sitting there after the game and taking in the beauty that can even be found in an artificial grass ball park. The crowd had pretty much filed out and they were closing the dome for the night.

"I wonder what Dad would have thought if he had ever had the chance to see this?"

I visited the Baseball Hall of Fame in Cooperstown by myself one summer. It was a good way to do it. I wanted to see if the magic was still there for me. It was. I laughed at some of the exhibits. I cried at memories. I refused to listen to the replay of the Boston Red Sox losing to the hated Yankees in a playoff game. I sat on the bench that Connie Mack of the long forgotten Philadelphia Athletics sat on. I did all the tourist things and loved it.

I bought some autographed souvenirs of my baseball hero Ted Williams. One of them hangs on my office wall. I brought back an authentic replica of a Brooklyn Dodger hat and gave it to Linda to keep for me.

I also brought back a couple of autographed Ted Williams baseball cards. When my nephew Mike was buried, he was a pretty good player and a great fan who was called away too early, I left one of my autographed Ted Williams card with him in his gravesite.

My Dad would have approved.

Jerry and the Window

When I was quite small, aged four through eleven, we owned a wire-haired terrier named Jerry. Actually my sister, Alice, claimed ownership of the dog but as the little kid in the family I had more to do with him than my sister did. I was certainly told that I was in charge of the dog anytime the animal got into trouble.

The wire-haired terrier by nature seems to get into trouble quite often. It would fight any dog that walked down the street no matter the size or breed. It would run off in any direction it chose, at the slightest whim. It would get a death grip on the poor dog that belonged to our next door neighbours, at least once a month, and hang on while frantic family members tried to disengage them by tail twisting, jaw prying and water throwing while all the while shouting instructions interspersed with threats to both dogs and to each other.

The dog once jumped off the porch roof when he spotted another animal on the street that needed attacking. Don't ask me how the dog got out on the porch roof but it involved a young boy trying to change the windows from storm windows to screens and leaving the window open and unattended for too long a period.

At any rate, he was not a vicious dog. He never attacked or bit a human but, had he been able to write, he could have written "The Territorial Imperative" as it applied to dogs. He was also never any good at learning how to open doors. The door knob was a complete mystery to him.

When I was quite small, aged zero to fourteen, I also had a father. Cancer took him away after an extended battle. Most of my thoughts and memories about my father have been positive. However, I recognized, even at a young age, that my father was not over-endowed with certain skills. One such skill that was almost completely missing had to do with any handyman skills that involved working around the house. As proof of the theory of genetics I am also totally lacking the same skills. The difference between my father and myself is that I recognize the fact but my father battled with it. It was a losing battle. He once replaced a screen in the back door by taking the door off its hinges and laying it down on the kitchen floor. He then removed the torn screen and laid out the new screen. The new screen was carefully nailed in place. When he completed the job, he went to pick up the door and discovered he had used nails that were slightly over-sized and that he had effectively nailed the door to the kitchen floor. Handyman work was not his long suit.

When we moved from Timmins to Hamilton my family was broke. Somehow, my father arranged a job as a line inspector in a defence plant and somehow they managed to get enough money together to buy a pleasant home in an older part of the city. They managed the home by renting out two small apartments and by living very carefully. Two couples of apartment renters, my father and mother, my sister and myself and occasionally my brother all shared one bathroom. Before one person took a bath it was ruled that they must first check with all other persons in the house at the time to see if the bathroom was needed before the facility was booked for bathing.

When I think back, that probably contributed to my need for regularity and certainly helped my scheduling skills.

The house was well built and it had a set of French doors between the living room and dining room. The French doors had rectangular windows of approximately 12" x 9" that were of opaque glass except for the bottom row. The bottom left hand window was missing from the day we moved into the house.

Our family always ate meals in the dining room. We weren't putting on the dog, so to speak, we just didn't have room in the kitchen for an eating table. From time to time, father would decide that we should shut off the living room during dinner and would close the French doors. Jerry, the wire-haired terrier, would still move from room to room by jumping through the open French door window.

One Saturday my father, the handyman skill challenged person that he was, decided he should repair the missing glass. He very carefully took measurements and set out for the hardware store to buy the replacement pane. Upon his return, he found that he had mis-measured and that the purchased pane of glass was too small. After a significant amount of muttering he returned to the hardware store with new dimensions and brought back another piece of glass.

During the installation process, while tapping in one side of the glass, an over-tap caused the second piece of glass to split up the middle. The second set of muttering from father was measurably louder than the first and I was able to confirm the correct pronunciation of a few words that I had been working on myself.

My mother had by this time, repaired to the back yard but my father only became more determined to get the job done and to get it right. Back to the hardware store for the third trip.

Watching this now experienced person putting the third piece of glass in place was a joy and a learning process that I thought I would never see. The glass slipped into place. The putty was stroked into a smooth reverse bevel. The glass was solid. The job was done.

Dinner was prepared and the French doors were closed so that we could all sit at the dining room table and admire the job that only took six hours and three trips to the hardware store to complete. Father was a proud and happy man. We were pleased to have survived the day.

The doorbell rung! Jerry, the wire-haired terrier leaped to his feet and headed for what had always been an open window. My father, my mother, my sister and myself all let out the same scream- "no Jerry no!" The dog arced gracefully through the air, through the glass and landed on the living room side with his paws straight up. We thought the glass had killed him. Then we thought that father would do the deed.

I don't know at times like that whether you laugh or you cry. The dog lived for another two years. My father lived for another three years and we lived in that house for another ten years.

The window was never repaired again.

Stories About the Stars

Unfortunately, or perhaps fortunately, there has never been a definitive book written about correct grandparenting. When I was astute enough to become a grandfather upon the arrival of Katie, I was thrilled beyond belief. When I was further astute enough to become a grandfather for a second time upon the arrival of Adam John (AJ) the cup runneth over.

As a parent it seems you are always concerned about the new arrivals. You talk the talk and you walk the walk but you're always a little on edge while you watch this little thing that you brought into the world struggle to learn everything that can be learned. You always feel just a little scared for yourself and for the new one.

As a grandparent, you feel an entirely different set of emotions. You're less likely to panic. The type of love that wells up is extra special because it contains your love and emotions and it also contains an understanding of the parental love that you see coming from your offspring who have now become Mom and Dad. The Louis Armstrong words from the song "It's a Wonderful World" that say:

"I hear babies cry, I watch them grow, They'll learn much more than I'll ever know", mists up grandparents something awful as they count the fingers and toes for the first time.

Wilford Brimley, playing a grandfather in the movie Cocoon, was just too perfect a grandfather. He spoiled it for the rest of us by looking so good at grandfathering and by saying exactly the right thing at the right time to his filmdom grandson. Those of us who don't look like Wilford or who don't have a good script writer just wing it as best we can without even having a grandparenting book.

As an old friend from Newfoundland used to say- "we can only doos the best we tries".

When my grandchildren were really small we used to trespass on the fancy golf course property to walk through the woods and find golf balls. I would get lost and Kate and AJ would set me straight so that we could find our way home. They would come home dirty with pockets full of golf balls to share and with stories about how we got lost but found the correct path home because "grampa told us to just follow our heart and we would be okay".

I was never very good at attending the hockey games and baseball games where they performed. Their parents were great with those things. We got them autographs from people that they might be impressed with or we took them places that we thought might be special.

We always bought more Girl Guide cookies than we should. We signed on for every sponsorship that came along. For years we shared Mass on Christmas Eve. I don't think they or their parents really understood why grampa's eyes welled a little at such times. Grampa never fully understood why it happened.

We took them on little excursions. We got to every graduation, first communion and confirmation event. We yacked on the phone occasionally. We read and listened to their stories. We told them stories. From time to time, we took them on little holidays.

We took them on a little fishing trip to Lake Nipissing. One of the great things about getting away from the city is that you can look up and see the stars. We did that a lot when we were at Lake Nipissing and when the mosquitoes let us spend any time outside at night.

I'm not much of an astronomer but on a really good night I can pick out the moon, Venus, the North Star, the big and little dippers and Orion the Hunter. Past that I defer to others.

Kate and AJ liked to hear grampa stories before they went to sleep at night. At least they said they liked the stories but they probably liked the extra stay up time that went with the stories. After a number of stories told during our trip I found the story well going a little dry. I started to scratch and stretch a bit to come up with new or different material.

One night I told them the story of Orion the Hunter and how Orion became a constellation of stars by chasing his foe across the landscape and making a great leap that carried him into the heavens where he can be seen to this day. It was embellished and it assuredly became a myth on a poorly told myth but it got me through another evening of story telling.

Grampa's are easy marks. Before AJ was old enough to take on a trip, we took Kate to Florida for a week. Near the end of the week when Kate and I were by ourselves on the beach I said to her, "Kate, you've been here a week. You've seen Mickey Mouse, porpoises, sand castles, sea critters, alligators, palm trees and all sorts of things. Of all the things you've seen, what have you liked the most?"

Kate answered, "Being here with you Grampa."

She's in the Will.

When we were at the end of our fishing trip I asked Adam, "of all the stories we've told during our trip which story did you like the best?"

Adam, who assuredly has some Irish blood in him somewhere said, "Grampa, I really liked the story about O'Brien the Hunter".

He's in the Will.

Go Fish

I once saw a sign on a pier that said "God does not subtract from one's lifespan the time that one spends fishing". Now that's a nice sentiment but based on that theory, pelicans should live forever.

Nonetheless, where sports like hockey, golf, football and lawn bowling might bring out the worst in a person, fishing often brings out the best. It's always easier to remember the incident than it is the place when one starts to think about fishing adventures.

For a number of years I was part of a group that flew into remote lakes to spend a few days away from everything other than fish and blackflies. You can only get a true sense of the size of Canada when you fly across it. Trains or cars can give you an added sense of space and the time it takes to cross but seeing lakes and bush until you run out of horizon can best be done from a plane. Seeing it from a very small plane makes it even more awesome.

We used to fly from Trout Lake over the Gatineau Hills to Lac LaGarde in Kippawa Park in Quebec. Six of us would fly in two pontoon equipped planes with carefully weighed luggage and more fishing tackle than you would find at the Toronto Sportsman show. One of the planes was piloted by Stan. Stan was an old bush pilot. He was just slightly over-weight, sported a crew cut and always had enough stubble on his face to qualify as a tough old bird. The other plane was piloted by a series of young pilots who wore wrap around sunglasses, hair gel, were clean shaven and wore cologne. There was a different young pilot each year. I think it was because Stan didn't like them and made sure they didn't last. We all wanted to fly with Stan.

Andy, Brian, Roy and myself were reasonably serious fishermen. Tom was a great guy to be with but needed some caretaking. John was very high maintenance and could put a hook in your ear as quickly as he could drop a frying pan full of cooking fish. He was one of those people who marched through life having a great time himself but leaving havoc behind him. The combination of Tom and John together in a boat was a frightening thought but, as we switched fishing partners around, had to happen from time to time.

They were fishing together one evening while the rest of us were in two separate boats on opposite sides of a nearby island. Sound travels well across water. My fishing partner and I thought we heard cries for help and started in that direction. Brian and Andy, in the other boat, heard the same thing and also headed towards the yelling.

When we rounded the point we discovered Tom bent over the side of the boat, up to his armpits in the water, desperately hanging onto his fishing rod, bent double, with the rod tip under the boat. John was sitting on the prow of the boat, as far away from the action as he could get, with his arms folded across his chest shaking his head. Tom was obviously tangling with a major sized fish and it was hard to determine, at first glance, which one was winning.

"Keep the tip up," yelled Brian from several yards away.

"Dammit", said Tom, "I knew that would be the first thing out of Brian's mouth. I can't," he wailed.

"What are you trying to do," one of us asked.

"I've got about a four foot pike on. I had it right up to the boat but when John saw how big it was he wouldn't let me bring it into the boat. He's been sitting up there, not helping me ever since."

"It's not coming into this boat," John growled.

The fish never did get landed in their boat. Roy and I somehow managed to bring it aboard our boat and left Tom to deal with his mutinous fishing partner. Things were tense in the camp that night but Tom was the hero.

On another occasion we were discussing some of Tom's problems while he was out of the cabin on an errand of nature. It was raining slightly and Tom was wearing a yellow rainsuit held up by suspenders.

"Just how bad is my Captain," asked the person scheduled to sail with Tom that evening.

Just at that particular moment, as if in answer to the question, Tom walked into the cabin. His suspenders were dragging behind and one of them caught on the closing screen door. Tom kept walking. The caught suspender kept stretching until it let go at full force catching the unsuspecting Tom in the back of the head.

"I've got my answer," said his sailing partner.

We never brought booze into the boats with us. We never got into the boats under the influence. We would, however, enjoy a pop after dark and, as fishermen have done since time began, we would sit around the fire as the night chill set in and listen to the wolves back in the hills answering the loons. Now when we see each other we re-tell the stories and feel badly because some of the old group has already passed along.

They're just fun stories and I hope the sign on the old fishing pier is correct so we can get to tell them for awhile longer.

Evils of Smoking

I stopped smoking in or about 1969. I started smoking when I was about fifteen years old. I bought a package of Sportmens cigarettes because I liked fishing and they had great pictures of fishing flies on their packages. I graduated to Sweet Caporal cigarettes because they had good packaging and you weren't considered quite the nerd as you were when you pulled out a package that had fish and fishing flies on it.

I hid the packages in the garage out back and carried them from my hiding place when I went out in the evening to check out the chicks and look cool. I failed miserably at both those endeavours, by the way.

I can't remember when I was busted and declared openly that I was a smoker. I do know that I gradually escalated the habit until I was smoking non filtered Phillip Morris at the rate of a package a day, plus four or five House of Lords cigars and carrying two pipes so that I could light up one when the other became too hot. Most of my shirts and some of my jackets were burned in one place or another. My fingers had that horrible deep yellow jaundice look and my teeth were getting more stumpy at each visit to the dentist.

We were working at a construction site that was at the bottom of a long but steep ramp. I had visited the site and was walking back up when I felt a tremendous pain in my chest and very quickly found myself fighting to take a breath. I was twenty-five years old at the time.

Not wanting to believe that I could possibly be having a heart attack I made my way back to my car, drove to the office and called my doctor. After hearing about the pain and knowing I was only twenty-five years old and it being a Wednesday doctor's golf day, he suggested that I take a Bromo and relax. After an hour I called him back to tell him that this was not a Bromo curable item and he agreed to meet me at my house on his way to whatever (see previous sentence).

When I arrived home, very much gasping for breath, I made my way to the couch to await the doctor and said to Wanda, "The first thing the doctor is going to tell me is to stop smoking. There's a pack of cigarettes in my jacket. Please get me one while I'm waiting".

There I was puffing away when the doctor arrived to deal with a person that had serious chest pains and couldn't breathe. I was hooked.

The doctor diagnosed the problem as a collapsed lung and told me that a couple of weeks of rest would allow it to re-inflate and, of course, told me to stop smoking. We were very busy at the time at work so rather than take two weeks away I took one week off and explained to the doctor that I had "double shifted" the healing process to get going again. I was smoking again a month later.

Aren't we really smart when we're twenty-five?

Like so many other smokers, I must have quit a hundred times. I finally reached a point where the burned shirts and jackets and the yellow fingers became bad enough that I made a very determined effort and stopped smoking for a period of about three months. I went cold turkey and it was horrible. I reached into my pocket ten times a day looking for a smoke but came up empty.

Addicts rationalize their habits. My excuse became the old "I'm putting on weight so smoking must be good for me in order to keep the weight down" excuse. We've all heard it and many of us have used it as a reason to not stop or to re-start.

I decided, after a particularly long and difficult day, to break the smoking fast by buying a small package of pipe tobacco and by promising to just occasionally enjoy a pipe of tobacco. I went home and after three months of non-smoking, lit up a pipe. It was great, but only for the first three minutes. I started to break a sweat. My body temperature felt like it had soared to 110 degrees. My stomach said, "That's the end of that."

I concluded from that experience that smoking was indeed bad for you. Besides, the price of a package of cigarettes had soared to thirty-three cents and we were on a tight budget.

Now, fast forward a few years to the time when our good son Dan reached the age of five.

Wanda and I were sitting at home one Saturday morning when Dan, who had been out with his pal, came home. He walked straight through the kitchen and down to his bedroom. He did not look well.

The telephone rang and it was Mrs. T., the mother of his pal.

"Is Dan home" she asked.

We said he was.

"Is he all right?"

"He looked a little strange. Why do you ask?"

"I just caught he and Matthew under the back porch smoking cigarettes" she replied.

"Thank you", we say. "We'll take it from there."

Down the hall we go to his bedroom. There he lies, looking just a little green.

"Who was on the phone," he asked.

"Mrs. T."

"What did she want?"

"You know perfectly well what she wanted" we responded. We then launched into the obligatory tirade against smoking. We included everything from stunted growth to fire hazards through to tooth damage.

Remember, we were talking to a five year old tad with curly hair and big eyes who knew he was in big trouble. He considered what we had been saying to him, as much as a five year old can consider anything his parents say, and then he said-: "Well, I only had one so it shouldn't be too hard to quit."

Don't laugh. It would be "unparental" to let on that the comment ended the story. Keep a straight face, at least until you have cleared the area.

Butch Cassidy

One of the great things about living in the country is that you have space around you and you don't need to bother with others or be bothered by them. Another one of the great things about living in the country is that you meet some great neighbours and you have some great times with them. They are also very helpful when they're needed and you get the chance to be helpful to them as well.

The main thing is there is more space and fewer people occupying it. That usually suited me just fine. When we bought our farm near Jerseyville it consisted of sixty-eight acres plus a powerline right of way, an old barn and the remnants of a small farm house that had burned down under mysterious circumstances.

I had no idea what to plant or how to plant it. Someone told me that oats were easy to grow so we planted oats. No one told me how much oats I would get or how I was to dispose of them when they were harvested or how, for that matter, to get them harvested. All I know is that by the time fall arrived I had oats everywhere.

We had figured out how to schedule a grain harvester to come in and combine the oats. We built the largest oat bin possible then figured out it would only hold approximately a quarter of the oats we had coming off the field. We had bought two old horses that were scheduled to eat some of the oats but we had no idea what to do with the truck loads that were coming off the field or what to do with the straw that was being produced behind it.

It was about that time that we met our next door neighbour Nelson. Nelson turned out to be a real nice guy. He was the poster boy for laconic. He was always the first person to show up when you had a snow plough stuck or a baler broken down or a seeder that wouldn't seed. He was just a good neighbour and it seemed that you never saw him unless you had a problem. Then, he would just magically show up. He was typical country.

At any rate, I was leaning against a fence post with a piece of straw in my mouth trying to look the part of the country farmer/rancher watching my first crop coming off. I was also trying to look calm even though I knew I had every storage area on the farm already filled with oats and had started to eye the basement of the house. I knew that, as far as the house was concerned, that if the oats went in Wanda would see to it that I went out. Nelson pulled up with his pick-up truck.

"Nice day" says Nelson.

"Yup" says I, chewing on my piece of straw and looking like a farmer/ranch, I hope.

"Good crop of oats" says Nelson.

"Thanks" says I, being very careful to keep the sound of panic out of my voice.

"People around here are starting to refer to you as the Oat King. What are doing with it all?" asked Nelson.

"I have no cotton picking or oat picking idea," I answered, starting to slip into panic mode.

Then Nelson spoke the magic words I was waiting to hear. "Maybe I could use some and maybe I could ask around to see if any of the neighbours need any?"

This was a long sentence for Nelson but it was music to my ears.

"Nelson, I'll pay you a commission or you can take a cut of the oats for your troubles or whatever you want", I tell him.

"Don't need to get paid", says Nelson. "I'll try to help you out." He did. That's what neighbours in the country are like.

As neighbours are fewer and further between, it's an event when someone new moves into the neighbourhood. We were still very much the new kids on the block but we were invited to a dinner at a neighbour's house to welcome a recently arrived new neighbour. The persons giving the welcoming dinner were also part time farmers. She was a full time joiner and organizer in the village. The host was a professor at the local University. His contribution to farming was primarily looking after a few rabbits in a back shed and using the rabbit shed as a place for Saturday afternoon naps and hiding out from his very busy wife with her job jar.

The new neighbour moving in was a dentist who had recently returned from a stint of dental service/missionary work that he had done with a group in South America. I was led to believe he had spent his missionary time in Bolivia.

The "Welcome to the Neighbourhood Dinner" would then be attended by some of our great farmer neighbours, some professorial individuals, gentlemen farmers and bozos like me. It would be an eclectic group indeed and, in some ways, a very intimidating group.

Having recently made a complete fool of myself with my oat crops and having demonstrated to almost anyone that might be watching, that my skills at working the land were entertaining but had little worth, I was determined to shine at the dinner and to restore my pride. I wanted to show that I was indeed a well informed person that would be worth while knowing. I set out to learn everything I could about Bolivia with visions of being the centre of the conversation that swirled about at the soiree.

I learned about Simon Bolivar. I learned that LaPaz was the Capitol City. Tin was a major export. I learned that Butch Cassidy and the Sundance Kid were reputed to have ended their outlaw careers in a shootout with the Bolivian militia. I learned things at the public library and through the Encyclopaedias that most Bolivians had long since forgotten or had never known. I was ready.

Dressed but not over-dressed, we strode confidently into the party. We were dressed casually chic so that we would not put off any of the guests by being over-dressed and would avoid any "down over the noses" looks from the professorial crowd. We were positioned right where we wanted to be. Let the impressing begin.

At the first appropriate moment I approached the guest of honour.

I introduced myself then moved to my opening sally with "I understand you spent a great deal of time in Bolivia".

"No" responded the doctor. "I spent all my time in Equidor."

Long silence. Long, long silence. I felt there was nothing to be gained by asking, "Where's Equidor and what do Equidorians do?" It's time to leave and make plans for my next oat crop.

Maybe we can have dinner together some other time.

How Do You Play This Game?

Casey Stengel, while managing the expansion team New York Mets, was quoted as asking, "Does anybody here know how to play this game?" The question came as three umpires and two managers were trying to sort out the situation where Stengel's Mets wound up with three men on third at the same time.

Golf is an even more amazing game with as many characters as there are golf balls. Each character, in turn, brings his or her own attitude, rules interpretations, style and eccentricities to every round that's played.

You have golfers who really don't care if they hit the ball long or short. You have golfers who get furious if they don't hit it long enough or short enough at any given time.

You have golfers who will take three minutes to carefully replace a ball that has been marked on the green and picked up for cleaning. You have golfers that will kick a ball ten feet away from a centuries old oak tree that might interfere with their direct line to the green and declare the oak to be a heritage tree, thus allowing them to move the ball.

You have golfers that speak in reverential tones while anywhere near a course and golfers that laugh and talk at decibel levels not reached at rock concerts.

You have golfers that line up a four inch putt from six different angles, then proudly tap it into the hole. You have golfers that will hit a thirty foot putt at warp speed, watch it run over the top of the hole and stop ten feet past the target. Those golfers are likely to invoke the "deemed to have dropped" rule that suggests that the ball, having passed over the hole, is deemed to have fallen into it, on the grounds that the laws of gravity supersede the laws of golf.

You have golfers that hate the game but play it every day, if possible.

You have golfers that love the game and seldom take the time to play.

Fortunes are spent on lessons, clubs, golf balls, gimmicks that remind you to turn your shoulders or keep your arm tucked in or your head down. None of it works. The best that one can hope for is to remember it's a game and the word "play" should be associated with the word "fun". That's not easy to do if you're a golfer.

To some of us, most of the fun of golf is taken from the ambience of the game, the time spent with friends, the use of the game as an excuse to get away from work or to take a holiday. In other words, most of the fun of golf occurs well away from the actual golf course. I've also learned over the years, the higher the intensity level, the lower the fun level. I also realize that to the golfing purist, this is a heretical position to take and to those, I invite you to continue to grind over those two foot putts and to successfully lower your handicap even if it means you can no longer speak civilly to your playing partners.

I'm a fairly intense guy. If you could look up the definition of "Type A Personality", you would find my picture.

Several years ago I was advised by a physician to take a certain medication designed to help me maintain a calmer disposition. They seemed to work. Then I found myself playing a round of golf. Our seventh hole has thick woods lining the entire left side. You hit from an elevated tee towards a green that is at the top of a long hill.

I teed up a ball and promptly slashed it deep into the woods on the left side, never to be seen again. As I try to stay ready for such emergencies, I took a second ball out of my back pocket, teed it up and promptly slashed it even deeper into the woods. Quietly humming a tune, I went to my golf bag and took out two more golf balls.

I teed up the third ball and deposited it somewhere beyond my second ball in the woods. I teed up the fourth ball and it was even worse. Then it struck me. I wasn't in the least bit upset. I had just hit four consecutive horrible golf shots and it wasn't bothering me. I should be really annoyed. There must be something seriously wrong. I figured it out.

I took the vial of calming type pills out of my pocket and placed them on the tee. I turned and faced the woods, took careful aim and drove the pill bottle into the deepest part of the ravine. That felt good. It was by far the best drive of the five I hit off that tee that day.

Golf should be a game and I'm trying to keep it that way. I still grump when things don't go well. I still bang an occasional club into the turf but I think I'm getting better at it. If there is any improvement in attitude, it's self- induced and not the result of a prescription.

I really don't know whatever happened to those pills after I hit my shot that day but I did notice some very mellowed out deer in the area over the next while and the fox didn't seem to much care if he did much hunting or not. They must have been powerful pills.

I Know That Guy

There is a theory that puts forward the observation that everyone in the world is only six touches away from everyone else. In other words you know someone who knows someone who knows someone etc. who, within six touches, knows the Pope or knows the Queen of England or Fidel Castro or all of them. It's an interesting theory and it may well be true.

Every time I try to test the theory in my own life, Larry and Marnie show up early in the six touches and they often reduce the touches to two or three. They know almost everybody or they know the person who knows all the other people.

I know Larry. Larry knows the President of the XYZ Company. The President of the XYZ Company knows the President of Mexico and that person knows Fidel Castro. Therefore, I'm within four touches of Castro. Marnie could probably speed up the process by two.

If you are walking someplace with them, leave lots of time. They will be stopped by almost everyone they encounter and you will be introduced to them. It takes time. If you want to know everyone in the room, go with Larry and Marnie.

Sometimes even the best misjudge.

Larry and Marnie were attending an event in Toronto and found themselves in the lobby of the Royal York Hotel close to midnight. There was a bit of a stir at the door and a white haired gentleman was seen entering at the head of a sizeable entourage. Ever curious, Larry made his way closer to the scene and announced to Marnie,

"I know that guy but I can't place him."

"You don't know him," responded Marnie.

"Yes I do. I recognize the face. I think I went to high school with him," insisted Larry.

"You don't know him, Larry. Let's move on."

"No, I'm sure of it. We went to Westdale High School together. I'm positive. I'll prove it," Larry said as he made his way toward the person he recognized as his old school mate.

"Larry, don't do it," Marnie warned. It was too late.

Larry, big grin in place with hand outstretched, marched up and announced,

"Hi! You may not remember me but I'm Larry. I'm sure we went to high school together but I've forgotten your name."

The somewhat startled gentleman stuck out his hand in greeting and said,

"Sorry, I don't remember you and I can't place the face." Slight pause. "I'm Johnny Carson."

Marnie just moved on and let Larry deal with the egg on his face. At least she now knows Larry who says he now knows Johnny Carson who, in turn, knows Ed McMahon and he knows the guy that owns Publishers Clearing House. The theory works.

Cooperstown

We were a family of baseball fans. Mike was, by far, the best baseball player but the rest of us tried to make up with enthusiasm what we lacked in talent. For years Mike and Marg's kids played sandlot softball. I coached Little League and Pony League teams. Dan coached Little League and representative teams with Adam as a player. We sat in major league bleachers and we sat in corner lot bleachers and enjoyed the game as players, fans, supporters and people who just liked to sit in the sun occasionally and bait an umpire.

Ironically, it was golf that caused me to go visit the Baseball Hall of Fame in Cooperstown. It was a visit that I always wanted to make but always had an excuse to avoid. I read an article by Steve Paikin who stressed the need to simply do the things that need doing. In his case it meant a visit to Cooperstown with his father, his brother and his son. It made an impression.

We belong to a very fine golf club. Many of our members feel that we need visits from professional golfers and professional golf tournaments to reinforce that it's a nice place. I know it's a great golf property so when our Board of Directors decided that we were to turn the course over to the Senior Golf Tour for a tournament I decided to take the opportunity to visit Cooperstown rather than hanging around watching a bunch of millionaires ride around in carts.

Cooperstown is a beautiful little town in upstate New York in the finger lakes district. I arrived late in the afternoon and found a bed and breakfast accommodation within walking distance of downtown and the Hall of Fame building. As I checked out the area, I was amazed at what was there that had nothing to do with baseball. There are museums, parks, an extensive summer opera program. There are even golf courses. The focal point, of course, is the Baseball Hall of Fame and I couldn't wait to see it.

The game and the attitude within the game has changed so much in recent years that it was a bit of a test to see if any of the old feelings about baseball would be re-kindled by having a good look at its history. When you visit the Hall, you are advised to take in the introductory film before you visit the exhibits. Take that advice.

When you first walk into the reception area, you are greeted by larger than life statues of Ted Williams and Babe Ruth. In the world of baseball, they are indeed, larger than life people. The introductory film opens with just the voices of young kids playing baseball. They were the same voices that I remember hearing when we gathered at Scott Park and chose teams or argued a call or re-aligned the teams to keep the game fair. They were the same voices I remember hearing as we tried to talk someone into staying and playing just a little longer or when offering the explanation that you had to go because you had papers to deliver or because you promised your Dad you would cut the grass before he got home. Yes, they play with your mind, but if you've ever been a kid on a baseball field, it's a great start to a visit with a part of your own life.

The average length of a visit to the Hall of Fame is, reputedly, approximately four and a half hours. I spent the four hours until closing time the first evening I was in Cooperstown. I was back at the opening the following morning and spent another five hours.

I visited all the rooms. I laughed at the St. Louis Cardinal pitcher that pulled strings during World War II to get re-assigned off General George Patton's staff and sent to the front lines because he thought he had a better chance of surviving. I sat on the bench used by Connie Mack as he managed his old Philadelphia Athletics in his street clothes wearing a straw boater. I walked out of the baseball radio broadcast exhibit because I couldn't bear listening to the announcer repeating the description of how a home run by Bucky Dent of the Yankees knocked my Red Sox out of a World Series appearance. My eyes blurred a little as I read a letter from Babe Ruth to a young lad in a hospital. It's corny stuff, but believe me, you come away feeling a lot better.

I spent the late part of the afternoon sitting in the bleachers at the small local field, watching two amateur teams play the game. The chatter on the field and in the stands had the same tone as the talk on the Hall of Fame film. That evening back at the bed and breakfast place, I sat in the parlour and exchanged the stories of the day's experiences with a young couple from Detroit and a director of one of the summer opera offerings.

The lady from Detroit had arranged the trip as a surprise birthday present for her husband. She pulled off the surprise to the point where they were half way to Cooperstown from Detroit before he figured out where they were going. It was hard to tell which of them was the more thrilled. The opera director was astonished that I could tell her about the pitching record of Cy Young and also discuss the works of Aaron Copeland and recognize both as American icons. Strangers became friends.

My favourite story about Cooperstown, and I hope it's true, involves an exhibit that none of us had seen. The staff at the Hall of Fame are constantly refreshing, cleaning and restoring various exhibits in the Hall. The story goes that they had removed one of the display cases for cleaning. When they were in the cleaning process, they found an old baseball card taped to the bottom of the case. It was not a major league player card but one of the locally produced cards that carried the picture of an unknown. There was a little information on the back of the card setting out the playing record of the pictured player.

The Hall of Fame staff, curious about how and why the card was found taped to the bottom of a display case, traced the card back to a small town in mid-West America. They identified the player and found his family.

When asked about the card, the player's son explained that his Dad had been a pretty good ball player. Unfortunately, he could never pursue a career in baseball as he had responsibilities towards his parents and then a family of his own to raise and support. He could never afford to take the chance of giving up his paying job in the local plant in order to find out how good he might have been. His baseball playing was limited to weekend games with the local team.

"I remember seeing him play when I was just a kid," explained the son. "To me, he was the greatest ballplayer ever."

"He loved the game," the son went on. "The only way he would ever be in the Hall of Fame, however, was if I put him there. That's why I slipped the card into where you found it."

The Hall of Fame staff, it's reported, put it back. I hope it's a true story.

Frisbees

Every now and again I pick up the paper or turn on the television and discover how someone has taken a very simple idea and made a fortune with it. Who would have thought that picking up a small rock, washing it and putting it in a box would cause it to become a "Pet Rock" and make a fortune for the genius that put the idea together.

The idea of taking a totally useless spring and setting it on a stairway so that it can fall down to the next step and be declared to be an expensive "Slinky" boggles my mind. How about the money that has been made over the years by taking a round piece of wood and putting it at the end of a string so that you can move it up and down? Isn't that clever? Or how about taking a heavier piece of wire and forming it into a large hoop so that thousands of people can spend big bucks buying the items and then trying to swivel their hips fast enough to keep the spinning hoop from falling to the ground? Another fortune made.

None of these ideas were that clever. A really clever idea, for example, would be the invention of the thermos bottle. A thermos bottle will keep things hot or will keep things cold. The really clever thing about the invention is someone having it programmed so that it knows which to do.

When we were growing up we were taught to respect the property of others. That doesn't mean we always did, but that was what we were taught. We also knew that when we failed to treat the property of others with respect, there could be a price to pay. In an age where a dirty look can bring on a law suit it's hard to understand a previous age where the destruction of another person's property may bring on a boot in the fanny from the offended party. We also knew that if we went home and complained about such treatment you generally received a similar boot in the fanny from the authority figure at home.

This doesn't mean that there was a lot of fanny booting going on but it does mean that there was a lot less stupid vandalism and wanton destruction. It also meant that lawyers did more meaningful work.

There was a very large man that lived about six doors down from our house on Prospect Street. He was an ex semi-professional baseball player and kept himself in pretty decent shape at that time. There were two sons in the family and we played back and forth and visited back and forth as kids. They were pretty good guys and their father, although a bit gruff, was a nice enough guy as well.

I went down to their place looking for the boys one day. They weren't home from school yet so I decided to hang out in their back yard until they showed up. I noticed that there was a ladder against the detached garage and that it appeared some work was being done on the roof. Being curious, I climbed up the ladder and saw that they were removing the old shingles from the roof and replacing them. I thought, "Maybe I can help".

I took one of the old shingles that was loose and flipped it off the side of the roof to the ground. I noticed that the shingle didn't just drop but caught a slight airdraft and soared a little before falling. I took another shingle and flipped it a little harder and aimed it a little higher. I got more soaring and more flight distance. A whole new world was starting to open up. This is how the Wright brothers must have felt at some time in their careers.

It was time for research.

"What effect would there be if I bent the shingle slightly along the edges and tossed it backhand?" I wondered. There was even more soaring and even more distance. This type of design and toss caused the shingle to clear the property of Mr. K. and land in a neighbours yard. I was on to something and I had a large supply of research material. I may have reasoned, if I reasoned at all, that the shingles all needed to be removed from the roof and sent to the ground. In my mind, I was only helping.

If the boys had come home from school on time that day I would not have got into trouble. Unfortunately, the time I had on my hands and the material I had to work with allowed me to strip about half the roof and deposit it throughout the neighbourhood. Did those shingles ever soar!

I was involved in my research to the point where I didn't hear Mr. K. climbing up the ladder behind me. He made his presence known by the solid boot in the fanny that we described earlier. I caught the ladder and hit the ground running for home. When I got home, somewhat out of breath and more than a little scared I was asked what happened.

I explained that I was just tossing a few shingles off Mr. K.'s garage roof when he sneaked up and booted me in fanny. Big mistake on my part. The next thing I knew I was being marched back to Mr. K. by my father and going through the apology routine and promising that I would be at their place every night, after school, until all the shingles that had been deposited around their yard and around the neighbourhood had been collected. Somehow or other I wound up with a sore fanny, a very annoyed set of parents and an unwanted project that took me a week to clean up.

A few years later I noticed some people in a park tossing a plastic disk back and forth. Some others were tossing plastic disks to their dogs. The disks would soar especially well if they were flipped backhand. The downturned edges caused them to catch airdrafts and stay airborne and allow long tosses. The disks were everywhere you looked. The Frisbee fad was in full bloom and someone was making a fortune.

I was onto that idea the day I climbed on Mr. K's garage. I had invented the Frisbee that day and no one knew or cared. I could have been a gazzilionaire instead of just being another kid with a sore fanny.

Maybe I'll invent something else. I should have applied for a patent on the Frisbee. Based on my early research, it was my idea.

Pot Roasts

When I was eighteen years old I had sworn off women for life. They interfered with playing baseball and hockey. They always had ideas that cost money on Saturday nights. They always needed a girl friend to accompany them to the washroom while you sat waiting and wondering what could possibly take an hour to get done. They wanted to go to dances and parties and all that stuff. They were impossible to figure out. I just gave up on them and decided that baseball held more promise.

I remember being trapped into going to a party one Saturday night. I would rather have driven matchsticks under my fingernails and have them lighted. Much to my good luck, hurricane Hazel roared through the area that day and evening. The call went out for volunteers to fill and stack sandbags at areas of the Beach Strip that were threatened by Lake Ontario that had gone crazy during the storm. There was a choice to make. I could dance and party or I could go out and risk being drowned. It was an easy choice to make, so I jumped into my car and drove to the Beach Strip.

For some reason or other it made me a hero, however temporary, among my peers. They felt badly that while they were partying, their pal was out risking life and limb. I really just thought it was the better option.

Ted and I were playing ball on the same team. He knew I had sworn off women but he told me of a girl he had met the week before at a CYO dance. He said I had to meet her and I agreed to show up the following week. She was beautiful then and still is now. It took me three weeks to ask her to marry me. It took me three years to organize the event but we were married shortly after my twenty-first birthday. She was twenty.

We raised three kids that sometimes made us crazy but more often made us proud. As of this writing, they are all still out of jail.

I hate Pot Roast. I don't mean to put down the beef industry but I hate Pot Roast. When we raised our own cattle I always insisted that the Pot Roast cut be turned into hamburger. Wanda agrees that a weekly hamburger has probably saved the marriage, so I have nothing against beef. I just hate Pot Roast. It ranks right up there with parsnips and brussel sprouts.

Wanda always let me work at what I wanted to do. She seldom calls me at the office and I've had the opportunity of setting my work hours and, therefore, sometimes getting home at odd hours. The habit of calling home before leaving the office has been in place since early in the marriage. I always ask what she has planned for dinner.

Every now and again, the answer to that question would be "Pot Roast". Occasionally, I would get a call and Wanda would say, "I'm thinking of getting a Pot Roast out of the freezer. Are you okay with that for dinner?"

My suggestion, in response, would invariably be that perhaps she should forget the Pot Roast and we would eat out that night. She worked the "Pot Roast in the freezer" scam for five years. I was either incredibly stupid or pre-occupied or both. Her plan came undone when our freezer conked out and I was helping her unload its contents before they spoiled.

There was no Pot Roast in the freezer. There was never a Pot Roast in the freezer. There would never be a Pot Roast in the freezer.

When someone was asked what he contributed the success of their marriage to be, he said he and his wife go out four times a week. She goes out Monday and Wednesdays. He goes out Tuesday and Fridays.

No matter what else is happening, Wanda and I make an effort to eat out every Friday. It all started over a Pot Roast.

Clearing Sidewalks

My parents, especially my Dad, liked the idea of entrepreneurship. I'm not sure they knew the word. I'm not sure there even was such a word when they were around. Justice Oliver Wendell Holmes once said, "I'm not sure I can describe pornography but I know it when I see it." That was the way my parents felt about entrepreneurship. I've tried to pass it along.

As a very little guy I got the first and eventually the largest Liberty Magazine route in our neighbourhood. I built it up. I got the first Hamilton Spectator route among my pals. I made and sold costume jewellery to raise Christmas money. I liked the entrepreneur thing. I was even the first one, among my pals, to go bankrupt. How entrepreneurish can you get?

We used to hope for snow, not so that we could have snowball fights, make snowmen, miss school or all those types of things. We hoped for snow so that we could shovel sidewalks and earn a quarter per house or get a whole dollar for shovelling the walks at a corner house. I used to make deals with three or four of my pals so that we could work together and get more of the big corner houses. That kind of wheeling and dealing goes on to this day. Now we call them mergers and acquisitions. The work, when done by a group, went faster and you eliminated some of the competition. I guess that was an early sign of entrepreneurship. Dad encouraged it.

People born in the mid to late thirties in Canada were very fortunate. We grew up in homes touched by the depression but we missed the War. Our war experiences consisted of having some awareness of sugar, butter, meat and gasoline rationing but no one was dropping bombs on us. I was born in 1936. By 1944, I knew what the lists of names in the papers meant but I didn't realize how much they could hurt. I knew that a blue star in the window meant that a son, daughter or husband was in the service. I knew that a gold star meant that someone wasn't coming back.

My brother Eddie, who was quite a bit older than me, went into the army. I remember visiting him at an army camp and being made to try on his steel helmet. I didn't like it. My oldest sister, Audrey, had a husband in the army. I liked his badges. My other sister, Alice, dated servicemen occasionally. My parents worried about that but as an eight year old, I couldn't understand why. After the war, she married an ex-serviceman.

People who served in wartime seem to only tell amusing adventure stories. They seldom talk of the scary times without considerable prompting and then it's without much detail. Archie, who married my sister Alice, told me of the time he was on a short leave in London. London was under the blitz with nightly air-raids and buzz bomb attacks. Buzz bombs were engine driven bombs that were designed to cut out over the City of London, drop and explode. They were extremely powerful and totally non-discriminatory. They got their name from the sound of their engines. When the sound stopped, you took cover.

Archie said he always had a great deal of trouble sorting out the pence, shillings and farthings that made up the British monetary system. He said he and his buddy were coming out of a subway station and he was counting a handful of change trying to sort it all out. Just as they reached the top of the stairs, a buzz bomb landed in the area. The concussion knocked the coins flying out of Archie's hand.

His buddy yelled, "run" and disappeared back down the stairs.

Archie said, "Run hell. You're talking to a man with Scots in his blood and I just dropped three beers worth of change."

He claims he recovered every last cent, then ran.

Another very good friend of mine, also named Archie, served as a thirty-four year old ensign in the U.S. navy in the South Pacific. He would very quickly gloss over his own tales of the South Pacific which included dodging Japanese kamikaze attacks and picking drowning sailors out of oil slick waters. He would delight, however, in telling about bringing an aircraft carrier up river to Falls River Massachusetts, at night under a full black out, calculating turns a mile in advance so as not to run aground.

I recently read the book "A Band of Brothers." It's the story of Easy Company, a part of the 101st Airborne Division that fought in Europe from D-Day through to the end of the European War. The book closes with a grandchild asking the question, "Grampa, were you a hero in the War?"

The veteran of Easy Company replied, "No son, but I was in a Company of heroes."

It seems to me there was a lot of that going around. We always stop and remember on November 11th.

When we went shovelling snow my Dad always told me that I could leave our house to the last so that we didn't miss any other shovelling opportunities. He also told me to make sure that I shovelled out Mrs. R's house first. He also told me that if he ever found me taking a nickel from Mrs. R, he would kick my fanny around the block. He didn't say fanny.

Mrs. R. had a gold star in her window. We never knew Mr. R.

Cabinet Minister

I met Joe when I was working as a desk clerk at the Royal Connaught Hotel. He was living in the hotel at the time while he looked for a house for his family who were still in New York. I learned that he was moving to Hamilton from New York to manage a construction company that specialized in deep foundations. Hamilton was a logical location because of the steel mills that often required such work.

I was working as a desk clerk having moved up from a job as a bell hop. I hated the bell hopping job. You earned your living by thanking people who gave you a quarter or fifty cents for carrying their luggage upstairs. Once, when I was on the bell hop job I roomed the entire football team from McGill University and then refused the tip proffered by the team coach because he once taught me when I was in high school. I didn't want him to think that I was doing that job as a career or even as a living. Pride sometimes makes you do strange things.

I didn't hate the desk clerk job. I only detested it.

At the time I met Joe I was trying to get into the radio broadcasting business. I had been offered a job at a St. Catharines radio station but the position was a few months away so I was desk clerking. Whenever I worked the 3:00 PM to 11:00 PM shift I would stay over and help the night auditors do their jobs. I never got paid for the work but I learned a considerable amount about the auditing and accounting business. It was a free education, in my mind, and the night auditors liked my efforts because it let them spend a good part of their shift napping or otherwise goofing off. Everybody was a winner.

It also gave me an opportunity to meet people such as Joe and when he offered me a job as an office manager, I took it. I thought that I could always switch gears when the radio job opened up but in the meantime I could take advantage of a short term position. I stayed for thirty years and eventually bought the company. On the other hand I gave up on my ambition to become a broadcaster and missed my chance to be Dan Rather or, more likely, Jerry Springer.

Joe was a New Yorker and an ex U.S. Marine. Both of those things carried a special aura in the late fifties. He was a great sales person. I brought some accounting skills and organizational skills to the party and together we got a lot of things done well. The Canadian operation, run by Joe and me, always seemed to do well. The New York operation was always struggling and treated our operation like a bit of a cash cow. They always managed to spend money a little faster than we could make it.

It didn't take too long before we figured out that a Canadian operation would have a better chance surviving on its own rather than trying to survive an ongoing New York cash drain. I convinced Joe to take the steps to repatriate the company and we became a Canadian firm.

In and around that time I increased my involvement in politics and eventually ran election campaigns for two different Members of Parliament and became quite involved in the local political scene. I always just worked behind the scenes but I was involved enough that some of the local politicians would answer my phone calls.

The company was reasonably successful and, as we were renting a considerable amount of equipment from time to time, I convinced Joe that we should establish a separate rental company and rent equipment to others as well as to our own company. The rental company was established with ownership in Joe's wife's name so that we could arrange additional financing and to make it easier to rent to other construction companies. The rental company was also successful.

Now comes the good part. I've been in business in one way or another since age sixteen. I've observed that one of life's biggest lies is the statement-"I'm from the Government and I'm here to help you." If you hear those words, run.

You can absolutely rely on the fact, however, that despite the fact that the Government cannot find any way to help small and struggling businesses they will find you immediately if you start making money so that they can collect as much tax as possible. That's what happened to our construction businesses as soon as they started to succeed. The tax department decided that even though the two companies were owned separately and provided separate services to different clientele, they should be taxed as one unit and pay more to help keep the Government flying first class. As this created a considerable cost and could have put us out of business we decided to appeal the decision to the tax department (we lost), then to the courts (we won).

We then discovered that the tax department with their infinite resources intended to appeal our court win to a higher court. I suggested that perhaps some of my political friends could be helpful in arranging a meeting with the Cabinet Minister to see if we could bring this matter to a close before the company went broke. We arranged the meeting.

I had always been under the impression that a Federal Cabinet Minister was just a person holding an important job. When our accountant and myself were ushered into the presence of the Minister I knew I had it wrong.

The reception area of the office was the size of a triple garage. The carpet was at least four inches thick. The leather chairs were real leather and designed so that you sunk slightly into them and were forced to look up at everyone. The secretaries were all prim. The administrative assistant to the Minister was stern. It was scary.

We had expected an "over the table" meeting with the Minister and had prepared a substantial number of documents that we hoped would make our case. A leather lined door leading to the Minister's office was opened and we were shown in by a secretary we had not yet seen. She closed the leather lined door leading to the outside office, then closed another leather lined door that led to the inside office. The office was the size of an airplane hangar. We walked into the Minister's presence on carpet that was now six inches thick. We had to pick our feet up and walk as if we were stepping through a deep bog. You could hear the silence.

The Minister sat at a huge desk on a slightly raised dais. He was puffing on the pipe that was his trademark. We were directed to low leather chairs that sunk even lower when we sat down. We sat there with our knees now at eye level with no work table in sight and tried not to be awed or intimidated.

The Minister had been briefed on the reason for our meeting. He asked me a few questions and in trying to answer them I wound up spreading my carefully put together work papers around my feet on the six inch carpet.

A few more questions. A few more papers spread. A few more questions followed by puff, puff on the pipe and a few more papers spread. Scattered would be a better word. A couple more questions followed by puff, puff on the pipe and more scattered papers.

I launched into my prepared comments about the values of repatriating a business back into Canada and the difficulties attached with starting a small business. I was just getting under full sail.

Very abruptly, the Minister got to his feet and walked in our direction saying, "I've got the picture. Someone from the department will be back in touch. Thanks for taking the time to come and see me." There was no offer of a handshake or of any other of the amenities one might expect at such a meeting.

I found myself clutching and grabbing at various piles of paper that I had spread out on the carpet. There was no time to sort them or put them away in an orderly manner. I grabbed papers, stuck some under my arm, handed others off to the accountant, clutched others in each hand and nudged my briefcase with my foot towards the leather door which had somehow magically been opened.

When we had cleared the inner sanctum and had a second to re-organize in the outside office I said to my accountant friend, "I get the feeling that we've just been tossed out on our ear by an expert."

"You have a great gift to sense the obvious," answered my friend.

No, Cabinet Ministers are not just people who hold an important job. At least this one wasn't.

We won the case so I guess he did get the picture and he sure left an unforgettable picture in my mind. He also helped hone my skills on how to end a meeting.

The Fence

Father Ray was a good homilist. I was raised a Catholic and spent summertime at Camp Brebeuf as a kid when my parents wanted to ship me out of town. They were not well to do but they made sure there was enough money for me to go to summer camp and stay out of their way. They must have really wanted to get rid of me because it was a significant sacrifice, on their part, to come up with the money to get this kid out of their hair.

Much of camp was fun. Unfortunately for me, I was a bit of a rebel and got into a fair amount of trouble at camp. For those of you who have not been paying attention, this probably explains why my parents would sacrifice to get me out of town.

Camp Brebeuf was staffed by seminarians that were studying for the priesthood. There are a couple of things that stand out in my memory about them. One, although most were great people there were some of them that were power trippers that made bullying their chosen sport and didn't seem to care who they scarred and two, we had to attend at a chapel service every afternoon where the seminarians practiced their sermons on a captive audience.

The first of these impressions caused me to stay away from the Church for almost twenty years before I got it figured out that the idea and the ideals are worth holding and that the individuals within such organizations are sometimes contemptible and must be worked past. The second Camp Brebeuf item caused me to try very hard to avoid the long winded and sanctimonious preachers that show up enamoured with their own words and voices.

Every now and again Father Ray announces that so and so will be preaching at the Masses next week and we all groan silently. Some of us groan not so silently as we consider the prospect of getting home next week after Mass and finding that the stew is over-cooked and that the timers have turned on our outside lights while we sat listening to the preacher.

Someone once told me that the brain can only absorb what the rear end can endure. That also explains why the Gettysburg Address is so famous. It took fewer than three minutes to deliver.

Father Ray was a good homilist. He was also a good enough person that my friend Ted and I started to invite he and another priest, a man that we had gone to school with, out to play golf once a year. One of the great things about arranging a golf game with a couple of priests is that we could leave it up to them to get us good weather as they were much better connected to the Big Guy because of their profession and could call in a favour.

After arranging and playing very delightful matches for three years in a row, Ted suggested that maybe we should miss a year. I opined that if he was expecting to have a Catholic funeral he had best put that idea out of his mind. He agreed and the games went on.

At any rate, Father Ray was a good homilist and a good story teller. Now from time to time, we would hear stories that we had told him, come back to us through one of his homilies. We had an occasional discussion about giving credits, paying royalties and about plagiarism in general but nothing came of it. Father Ray continued to tell his stories and we generally got out of Church at a decent time.

He would tell stories as part of his homily and use them to segue into a message. He told the following story and used it to talk about tolerance, loyalty and friendship.

He told of France in World War II and of a group of flyers that was always faced with the fact that their life expectancy was short and that friendship was very dear. Usually when people were assigned to their tent of four it was to replace the friend that didn't return from the last mission. The turn-over of people was so great that there was little time to get to know anyone and you were left with first impressions only, but you learned to recognize good people very quickly.

One such person did not return from a mission but his body was recovered and returned to the air base. His three surviving fellow flyers wanted to arrange a proper funeral for their fallen comrade and approached the local Catholic Church pastor and asked for permission to have their friend buried in the local Catholic cemetery beside the Church.

The priest explained that as they had no idea of the religion of the slain flyer and as there was no way of determining whether or not he was a Catholic, it was impossible for him to allow the burial of their friend in the Catholic cemetery. He knew, however, how deeply the men felt about the situation and he knew that the deceased had given his life fighting for someone else and that something needed to be done. He offered to perform a burial service but explained that the actual grave would be located just outside the fence of the cemetery.

Feeling this was the very best that could be done and recognizing that the priest wanted to do everything he could do to accommodate the request, the men buried their friend.

Several years later the three men, having survived the war, returned to France together for a visit and went to the village to pay their respects to their friend. They searched the burial area outside the fence but couldn't find any evidence of the gravesite. They visited the local priest to inquire about what might have happened and were directed to the retired old priest, now living in the village, to see if he could shed any light on the mystery.

The old priest recognized them and remembered the entire episode very vividly.

"I knew how strongly you felt about doing the right thing for your friend" he told them. "I knew how much it meant to you."

"I really agonized over the situation and agonized over the rules that caused it. After the war moved on and ended, I spent a great deal of time researching the rules and studying the Church Canon Law that governed such situations."

"After doing all the research I felt I could do, I found absolutely nothing in the laws and regulations that prevented me from moving the fence. Your friend is in the cemetery where we buried him in 1944. The fence is just in a different place."

Father Ray was a good homilist.

Summer Job

When I was a kid, organizing a summer job very often meant creating the job yourself. The job usually consisted of putting together a paper route or selling magazines door to door or entering into a lawn cutting arrangement with a few neighbours. More often than not it was a combination of some or all of the foregoing.

As you got older and, if you were really fortunate and your Dad worked in one of the mills, you got a student job in the mill and made big bucks. Some of the really lucky guys got jobs picking tobacco in the Simcoe area. Those tobacco jobs are now all filled by immigrant contract labourers because we find the work too hard. You could also make some money picking fruit in the late summer but there weren't any Hortons or McDonalds that provided entry level jobs and experience.

I think it's great when I see kids holding down those kinds of jobs now and learning about life. I think it's sad when I hear kids disparage those kind of jobs because they feel work of that nature is somehow beneath their dignity. I guess they're waiting for someone to come along and offer them a job as a bank president or something more in keeping with their skills.

I spent one summer as a service person at Camp Brebeuf. I had been sent to that camp as a camper and perhaps I had given them a bad enough time that the powers that be thought they could get even by offering me a service job when I got older. It didn't pay much but it kept me out of trouble. It also ruined my taste for rice pudding, which was served four times every week.

Bob Waller and I spent another full summer operating an outdoor bowling alley at a summer resort in the Muskokas. We were sixteen at the time and there was much to learn. Again, the pay was light but we were well fed and we spent the entire summer outdoors. We had the opportunity of learning much about the ladies. The guests on weekends were divided about evenly between male and female. During the week, however, there were considerably more females than males at the resort. Even the dumb sixteen year old males were "encouraged" to attend all the dances and otherwise stay sociable. With all the opportunities available to fish, swim, canoe, bowl and explore I found such "encouragement" an imposition on my personal time and avoided such occasions whenever possible.

Someone once said that Yasser Arafat never missed an opportunity to miss an opportunity. I know now what that means. I also grew to hate Nat King Cole songs that summer. He had several hits and his songs were on the resort recreation hall juke box. As there was a complete turnover of guests every week, there was no need to ever change the songs on the juke box. As we were there for eight consecutive weeks and heard the same songs over and over, we came to hate the sound of his voice.

I once worked for the Coca Cola company as a delivery helper on the trucks. The product was delivered in wooden containers and most of the deliveries were made to small stores and into basement storage areas. I would lug the full containers off the truck and load them onto a wheeled dolly. The dolly would be pushed to the top of the basement stairs and I would then lug two cases at a time down the stairs. It was my job to carry the empties back up the stairs and load them back onto the truck. While all this was going on, the truck driver would usually be sitting on a stool carrying on a conversation with the store owner while he made out the invoice and collected the cash. I weighed about 130 pounds at the beginning of that summer and 115 pounds at the end of the summer. I went home and hurt every night but it made me very determined to not go through life lugging stuff for a living.

While I operated our construction company I tried to make an effort to hire one or two summer students. It gave them a chance to make a decent dollar and to see a little bit about what makes the world go around. Dan reached the age where he was looking for summer work and it made sense for him to work for the construction company. We hired he and his pal Tim as light work labourers and gofers when they were about sixteen and put them to work on a project in one of the steel mills.

We were driving pipe piles in a large grouping, or mat, for a new mill project. We wound up with 200-300 pipe piles all lined up in rows in a rather deep excavation. The pipes all extended two to three feet above the bottom of the excavation and were all cut off at the same level. The piles were to be filled with concrete but the inspectors would not allow us to fill them until all the piles were driven in the area. They were concerned that the vibration caused by driving a new pile might damage the concrete in a pile already driven. They also registered their concern with the owner over the possibility that, if it rained, rainwater might get into the uncovered piles. They demanded that the open piles be covered. Inspectors like to make demands like that because it isn't their money being spent to comply.

After considering a number of ways to temporarily cover the piles I hit upon the idea of getting plastic garbage bags and putting one over the top of each exposed piece of pipe. It was a good idea, I thought, and the price was right. I explained what I wanted done to Dan and Tim and sent them out to buy a supply of garbage bags and to get the covering done. It was a full days job for the two of them. I didn't realize until I stopped by the jobsite late that afternoon that they had purchased the smaller white plastic bags and had used them to cover the piles.

From the top of the bank of the excavation it looked like a row upon row Ku Klux Klan rally. The boys had very carefully lined every bag up so that the pointy little ears were all in a row and every Klan member was facing in the same direction. Within an hour, the jobsite had become a major tourist attraction for everyone in the plant. It had also become a major insult, as far as the owners and inspectors were concerned, and I answered every one of the sixty calls I received over the next hour with the words, "I know. I know. We'll get it fixed." Once more I was a legend.

There is an old saying that goes, "God looks after drunks and dumb Irishmen." I seem to fit one or the other or occasionally both.

That night nature came to the rescue. We had a major cloudburst that caused most of the Klansmen hoods to fill with rainwater and collapse down the open piles. The piles we were trying to protect against water intrusion now had water and a white plastic bag in them but at least the rally had been broken up.

The phone calls started again with instructions to get those plastic bags out of those piles. At least they had now become so concerned about the Klan rally, the tourist site and the fact that there were plastic garbage bags in the piles that they had forgotten to worry about water. All I had to do is figure out how to get 200-300 plastic bags out of twelve inch pipes at a depth of anywhere from three to sixty-five feet.

The next morning people driving by the job site were treated to the picture of my two summer students, Dan and Tim, wielding short fishing rods with triple gang hooks attached. They would drop the line down the pile, fish and flail until they hooked a bag and then reel it to the top. A successful hook-up would invariably bring the shout "I got one" from one of the fishermen. At sixteen, it's a lark.

The project went on for some weeks. Workmen would stop by to see how they were biting or whatever. It was a good summer job for a couple of good kids.

Four Lads

Long before Led Zeppelin or the Rolling Stones or even the Beatles, kids were enjoying and trying to mimic music groups. This tradition probably goes back well past Barber Shop Quartets and probably reaches back to the time when travelling minstrels or Psalm singers entertained in tents and castles. It does go back to a point where the words that were sung could be understood. Every generation has made the same observation. "When I was a kid, the music made sense." That will never change.

Mimicking musical groups has never stopped the "tonally challenged". The situation of finding oneself tonally challenged is usually handled by singing more loudly. I stopped singing out loud a long time ago except for those few occasions where a few notes are part of a story I am telling or if I get caught up in the moment and sing along with several thousands of others at an event where they are doing the National Anthem. I have the feeling I can hide.

My singing career ended early. When I was in the second or third grade at St. Ann's school in Hamilton I found myself selected to be part of the Christmas Concert Opening Chorus. I didn't realize, at the time I was selected, that the Nun doing the selecting knew that I owned a suit jacket. I have no idea how I got the jacket. It certainly wasn't because I was a clothes horse or because my parents had so much extra money that they decided to buy me a jacket. All I know is that I owned a jacket and that I was in the Opening Chorus at the Christmas concert.

After the first rehearsal I was told to sing more softly. After the second rehearsal I was told to sing even more softly. After the third rehearsal I was told by the Nun to just mouth the words and not sing at all. When I asked what, then, was I doing in the Opening Chorus, I was told that they needed my jacket and, unfortunately, I came with it. Teaching Nuns may have been well meaning but they were never too subtle.

Not many of us, even those who are non-singers, need to search too far or too deeply in ourselves to find songs that have affected our lives and that cause old scenes and old memories to very quickly spring to life. I think that's a good thing.

Tammara had completed her final year in High School and had been accepted at the University of Guelph. She was leaving within a few days to take on another adventure and step in life. We were clearing straw off a back field on our farm and the entire family was working together to get a job done before the sun went down. It was a beautiful late summer evening and we were at the end of a long day of hard work. The sun was just starting down and we were loading the last bales onto a pick-up truck. Linda pushed the bales together, Wanda drove the truck, Tammara and I were walking along and tossing the bales up to Dan who was stacking. The truck radio was on and the song that was playing was "The Way We Were". Life was starting to change but an indelible memory was etched into my little brain.

You have your own thoughts and memories and music is probably part of them.

My good friend Ted and I have known each other forever. From time to time, we would drift apart or find ourselves on different paths but each always knew the other was out there somewhere and could show up at anytime as a friend. Our musical singing group was the Four Lads. For those not familiar with them, the Four Lads were four guys that had attended St. Michaels College and sang in the St. Mikes choir together. They formed their own group and were the big Canadian singing heroes of their day.

Ted and I and our group, including our future wives, attended Four Lads concerts, bought their records and knew their every song. As we could understand the words, we would sometimes try to sing them. Actually Ted and George and Bill tried to sing them. I just mouthed the words having learned my lesson from the Nun in the days of the Opening Chorus at St. Ann's.

We knew all the songs. The Mocking Bird, Dance Calinda, Those Wedding Bells are Breaking Up That Old Gang of Mine, Istanbul and the song that became my favourite, Moments to Remember.

Moments to Remember started with the words:

"The New Year's Eve we did the town" and moved through other thoughts of football games, prom dances, quiet walks and noisy fun and so many other things that we touch on but don't recognize as being important until we have passed by.

"When summer turns to winter and the present disappears,

The laughter we have always shared will echo through the years", tells the story that we too often miss. Corny? I guess. But that's okay.

I had left school to pick up some slack at home and Ted had been accepted into the most prominent business course offered at Western University in London. I volunteered to drive his stuff down to Western on move-in day. Wanda and Ted's wife to be, Marianne, went with us in my 1947 Monarch. It wasn't a bad car. It had a few dents and a balky fuel pump and two questionable tires but it had a good radio.

We were at another point where the paths would diverge. Ted became the head of a major Canadian corporation. I followed a different trail. We both cheered for each other over the years and took pleasure in the successes of the other. We both felt the pain of the other's troubles or failures.

We drove onto the campus at Western and found the residence. We were sitting in the car for a few minutes before we started the job of unloading and the Four Lads came on the radio with "Moments to Remember". This is not a bad B Movie script. This happened and it wasn't an easy moment.

I had the opportunity of putting something in front of Ted and Marianne at their fortieth wedding anniversary. I was out of town at the time and could only present my thoughts by letter.

I just wanted to remind us all of where we had been and where we had come from and how we had arrived at wherever we are now. The words sung by the Four Lads so many years ago were really helpful in telling how I felt. I especially liked the line- "The laughter we had always shared, will echo through the years."

It probably was just as well that it was done by letter. I would have had a lot of trouble getting through those memories if I was there in person. We all mark our own thoughts in different ways.

Raising Vealers

One of the goals I had in life as a young man was to be a rancher, raise cattle and write the great novel. It sounded like such a good idea and ranching always looked so good in the movies and on television.

They never showed frozen pipes in barns or tractors that wouldn't run or cattle that would run. They very occasionally showed a stampede but that was just to get the greenhorn killed or to show how truly evil the rustlers were when they were trying to steal your livelihood.

At any rate, I decided that it was time to buy a farm and to live my dream. Wanda agreed reluctantly to the deal with the proviso that the farm not be more than ten minutes drive from the town where we lived. I bought 45 acres of hills. It had an old broken down barn with an even older and more broken down shed. It also had an even older and more broken down house that was rented by a family of four.

Dave, the tenant, had two little kids and no money but he talked a great game as a farmer and handler of livestock. I had very little money after the farm purchase and absolutely no experience as a farmer other than those I had dreamed as a kid.

Dave convinced me that if I bought a dozen very young calves and put them in the shed and if I bought the feed for the calves that he would look after them in return for half the profit made at their sale. It sounded like a can't miss plan to me.

I found a nearby farmer and asked him to find me a dozen "vealers" and get them delivered to the farm. That was done and, in the meantime, I had purchased the proper feed and supplements at the local feed meal and delivered them to Dave. Dave and I sealed the profit sharing arrangement with a handshake.

Once twelve calves were turned into a pen together I couldn't tell one from the other but I could count to twelve. As we had not yet started to build our house on the property I left my herd in the hands of my "hired hand".

About a week later I got a telephone call from Dave.

"Pat, I've got some bad news. One of your calves has died."

"What happened?"

"It came down with the scours and died. They go fast at that age."

Concerned about my own health, I asked "what the hell is scours".

"Well" drawled the hired man putting on his best I know what I'm doing but you city guys don't, kind of voice, "it's like a kind of dysentery and it takes them down fast."

We agreed on a type of very expensive medication and further agreed that if I gave him the money he would see that the herd got the medication. He got the money the next day but I'm not sure if the herd ever got the medication.

At any rate, I got another call a couple of days later.

"Pat, more bad news. Another one of your calves died". It was the same story and the same set of problems. "They go fast' declared Dave.

Three days later I got the third call.

"Pat, you lost another one of your calves to the scours".

"Wait a minute," I said. "I keep hearing how I've lost another one of my calves. You understand that we are losing our calves when they die. I'm not losing my calves."

"Oh no" replied Dave. "When those critters came in here we each owned half, just like you said. That means I owned six and you owned six. Three of yours have died and my six are doing fine. I know which is which."

Now, I'm just a city bumpkin but even I can catch on to when I'm being taken for a long walk in a small meadow by a country slicker. I got out to the farm the next day with the intention of shipping out the rest of our quickly diminishing herd and found that my man Dave had arranged to have his brother pick up the calves and take them to market. It sounded very close to rustling to me.

We arranged our own calf transport after asking an OPP officer to explain that the brother shouldn't have the calves in his truck without proof of ownership regardless of how well brother Dave knows their names. We went to market. We sold the vealers. We split the proceeds, after expenses, evenly. This meant that neither of us got any money when the cost of the animals had been paid. I got out of the vealer business real fast and my hired hand was invited to seek residence elsewhere.

I lived on farms for about fifteen years and never learned how to tell one piece of beef on the hoof from another. Dave was one of the only people I ever met that could pick out his calves from mine, especially when they were dead.

I did, however, learn to value the comment once made by Cecil B. DeMille, the movie mogul. "A verbal contract isn't worth the paper it's written on."

General DeGaulle

I had never been to Quebec City. When I was fairly new to the construction business we decided we would bid on a Provincial project in the Province of Quebec. This was back in the days before coloured television and before the days when the Province of Quebec would only deal in French.

Although the project was being done in Sorel, PQ, the bidding took place in the Quebec Capitol, which, of course, is Quebec City. This meant that the tenders needed to be delivered to the Department of Public Works in that City. I was chosen to deliver the Tender so off I flew to Quebec City armed with my High School French.

The people of Quebec do have a very different attitude than the people of Ontario with our buttoned down collars and our buttoned down minds. For example, Quebec people actually sing in public without being drunk. They talk to each other on the streets and in elevators. They wear colourful clothes. All these things were a total revelation to this little Ontario boy.

There were also other revelations that came to me as my experience with Quebec increased over the years. I once had a hotel room in Sorel that was on the main floor of the building. I came out of my room and was passed in the hall by a beautiful young lady in briefs and bra. I lingered. Before long I was passed by another and then another. It seems there was a lingerie fashion show taking place and the models were changing in a room down the hall then going on into the show wearing very little other than a smile. I liked my room location but when I asked for it again on my next trip I discovered there were two stags and a presentation being made by Amway that night. Oh well.

Expo67 worked because it was held in Quebec. The joie de vivre is there. Expo67 could not have worked in Toronto, even though Torontonians believe with all their hearts they are the center of the universe.

Quebecers love pageantry provided it has nothing to do with the British Monarchy. The British love carriages and large horses clopping along wide avenues. Quebecers love bright tunics, shiny helmets and loud motorcycles. They also really loved General Charles DeGaulle. Churchill described Charles DeGaulle as the Cross of Lorraine and his cross to bear. Roosevelt described DeGaulle as an S.O.B. but our S.O.B. Quebecers, on the other hand, had him up there with the Deity.

I had no idea that Charles DeGaulle was scheduled to visit Quebec City on the same day I was scheduled to deliver the Tenders. It was an overnight trip for me because of plane schedules and I was fortunate to have reserved a room in the great old Chateau Frontenac Hotel. It's a beautiful old hotel that over-looks the St. Lawrence River and the famous boardwalk.

Because I had no other real business to attend to other than making a delivery, I spent some time exploring the City and doing tourist things. The Chateau Frontenac opens onto a cobble stone courtyard with buildings on three sides and an archway entrance. An enclosed area, such as this, tends to amplify noise and the rumble of engines bounced off the walls and had drawn quite a crowd.

I discovered DeGaulle was in town when I returned to the hotel and found the courtyard filled with Mounties in dress uniforms and Quebec Provincial Police in shiny white helmets sitting on their motorcycles revving their engines. Revving engines in a very close space with three walls creating echoes makes a very impressive sound. It also was making the QPP people very happy. They explained that DeGaulle was attending a meeting with the Quebec Premier and that they would shortly be going to the Premier's office and escorting the General back to the Chateau when the meeting ended.

I went up to my room and showered and headed out to have dinner. I was alone in the elevator and when the elevator doors opened onto the lobby I was faced with two lines of police officers stretching from the elevator doors to the main entrance. They were standing motionless but at ease. There was a QPP Officer, then an RCMP Officer, then another QPP Officer and so on out to the door. A large crowd had gathered in the lobby awaiting the momentary arrival of DeGaulle.

Out stepped the little guy from Ontario.

"Mon Dieu", I thought. "Quescque c'est?"

At that point some wag in the crowd spotted me and started to applaud. The rest of the people immediately took it up. I bowed in their direction and bailed out a la gauche.

There have been a lot of strange things happen in Quebec. Over the years there has been a lot of tension and a number of problems but I can always remember the great reception I got as a young man from Ontario with a police honour guard provided by two levels of Government and an appreciative audience. I don't think General DeGaulle did any better.

Ropes

There are a number of old sayings about ropes.

"Give a man enough rope and he'll hang himself" and "I sure got roped in on that one" are two that very quickly spring to mind. I've had experience with both.

One of the pieces of good advice I was given when we started to keep horses on our farm was that as a horse is a very big, strong, tough animal that is often at one end of a rope while you are at the other end of the same rope, there are times when you better know enough to let go. I had heard that advice and felt, that being a reasonably intelligent person, I would recognize such situations and behave accordingly. From time to time I have seriously over-estimated my own intelligence.

When we started to deal with horses we were on a learning curve that seemed to go straight up. As we took up riding horses we also found ourselves on horses that seemed to go straight up or that saw to it that we left their backs and went straight up. The first horse I ever bought was a sour old plug named Suzy. As long as you left Suzy alone, she left you alone.

We had been sold the horse because we wanted something that was easy to ride and that would be good for the children to work with and learn. Suzy was about eighteen years old, which is a good settled age for a horse and wasn't overly big so we felt the kids could get on her easily and do some rudimentary riding. I noticed that she kept her ears very flat and assumed that was because she was attentive to those sitting on her back. I didn't learn, until after the payment cheque had been cashed by her former owner, that flat ears really indicated that the horse was angry and would kick you in the shins in a moment, given the chance.

I learned about her moods very quickly. She only had one. Mean. I figured out that most horses kick straight backwards so that as long as I stayed out of the direct rear direction I should be okay. Suzy taught me that some horses can "cow kick" which means that they kick to the side rather than kicking to the rear. I found that out by standing beside Suzy and not paying enough attention. The rap I received on the shins healed in about two weeks but the lesson remained forever.

We were also warned by her former owner that we should never hit Suzy but that it's a good idea to carry a stick with you when you're riding and "show her the stick" if she decides not to go when you want her to move. One day, early in our ownership, Tammara was up on Suzy and Suzy had declared by planted feet and flat ears that she was in no mood to go anywhere. I told Tammara to show her the stick. It didn't help. I decided to get up on the horse with Tammara and I would make her go. I was no sooner in the saddle when Suzy went straight up in the air and I was off her and deposited part way across a nearby fence. Tammara was demonstrating her bronc riding abilities and hung on until Suzy settled down.

When I asked her former owner about the explosion he advised, "Never try to ride double on Suzy. It's one of the things she doesn't like." I put that dislike down on the list along with the forty other dislikes we had already discovered.

We had a blacksmith come to the farm to do some shoeing on Suzy. He was standing beside Suzy getting ready to start his work when he discovered that Suzy "cow kicked" to the side when she wasn't happy. Having already ascertained that Suzy was always likely to be unhappy, he left without doing any work. I couldn't blame him.

A neighbour told me about another blacksmith that lived about five miles away but that we would need to take Suzy to his place as he didn't make house (horse?) calls. We didn't have a horse trailer at that time but he offered to drive us over with me sitting in the back of the pick-up truck and Suzy walking behind at the end of a rope. It seemed like a workable idea to me but, in retrospect, it was another one of those ideas that I didn't think through.

The early part of the walk was easy. Jim drove at about three miles an hour. I sat in the back with my feet hanging over the lowered tailgate and Suzy clumped nicely along behind. Jim got a little bored with the pace and slipped up to five miles per hour and Suzy went along with that change. Jim increased his speed very slightly. I tightened my grip on the rope. Suzy decided that even five miles per hour was too fast and went to a dead stop.

It's a terrible feeling when you have a wrap around grip on a rope attached to a thousand plus pound animal that has come to a complete stop and you feel the truck you are sitting in moving on out from under you. Fortunately, not too many people have had that feeling. I did.

Jim must have gone another quarter of a mile before he checked his rear view mirror and saw that his load was missing. I wasn't about to move without the assistance of a chiropractor so he found me sitting on the road and Suzy very contentedly munching grass in the ditch but still at the end of the rope. As far as she was concerned, she had done a good day's work.

I had another memorable experience with a rope when myself and three friends were driving north on a fishing trip. I had come to a stop behind a pick-up truck that was carrying an aluminium row boat. The prow of the boat was facing the rear of the truck with a rope trailing from the lowered tailgate.

Totally unbeknown to me, when I stopped behind the pick-up truck one of my front wheels had stopped on the rope. When the pick-up truck pulled away, the row boat was left behind on the road and in front of my car that was still parked on the rope.

The pick-up truck driver slammed on his brakes and exploded out of his cab waving his arms and telling us what complete jerks we were to have unloaded his boat the way we did. I suggested that before he totally alienated a car full of people who represented his only hope of re-loading his boat, that he try to be nice to us. He settled down and we reloaded his boat and sent him on his way a chastened but wiser man.

I should have known about ropes early. At a very young and impressionable age I watched my father trim a large branch off a tree in our backyard. The limb over-hung a neighbour's fence and thus, couldn't just be lopped off and allowed to fall.

My father tied a rope to the limb to be trimmed and tossed the rope over a higher branch so that the loose end fell to the ground.

"When I've cut the limb, hang on to the rope so that you can just lower the branch to the ground" he instructed my sister Alice.

The cut was made. The limb came down and Alice, dutifully hanging on to the rope as she had been told, went straight up.

There are two lessons to be learned from this last story. One, don't expect a girl that weighs one hundred pounds to hold up a three hundred pound limb. Two, there are times when you better let go of the rope.

The Ping Pong Club

When we bought our first house we were as poor as the proverbial church mice. We had three mortgages and I had one job for each mortgage. We even made a deal with the builder, in order to reduce costs, that we would paint the inside windows ourselves.

As I felt the application of masking tape before the painting was too time consuming, I painted the frames with the thought that I would scrape any mistakes off with a razor after the fact. We wound up with a lot more paint on the glass than on the frames and this brought a very irate builder to our door demanding that the clean up be done "right now" as his reputation was in serious jeopardy because of my unsteady paint hand.

Suffice it to say that we had no money and not much likelihood of having any disposable income in the near or intermediate future.

When you're broke you find ways to entertain yourselves. Everyone in our new survey was in the same position. We all had one to four children, big mortgages for the time, relatively new jobs, a ton of responsibility and no money.

A group of the men decided that we would start a ping pong club and each week go to a different person's house on Monday night and play ping pong. We helped each other build or assemble ping pong tables and the deal was on. Actually, we reached a point where we were playing a fairly decent level of ping pong. It was a cheap and easy night out. The dutiful wife at each location would put together a little lunch and it was a fun thing to do.

The competition would sometimes get a little fierce but we had a good time.

The players were all from the same survey but we were approached by a person from another survey that wanted to join the club. Fred was a very pleasant man but was light years removed from having movie star looks. Actually, he was altitude challenged, had a mop of totally unmanageable hair, ears that stood straight out giving him the look of a taxi cab going down Main Street with both doors open, and he was as round as he was tall. Other than that, he was a good looking guy a nice fellow and a decent ping pong player.

As our group rotated from house to house each week, we got to the point where the games were to be played at Fred's house. None of us had ever been there before and none of us knew anyone in his family.

On ping pong night, four of us rode over to Fred's place in the same car. Another one of our members drove his own car as he was going to be a little late. We found Fred's house and rang the door bell. The door was opened and we were greeted by an absolutely gorgeous woman. She was tall. She was slim where she wanted to be slim and not so slim where she was pleased not to be slim. She had long red hair, a face that could win a cover girl contest and a smile that would stop a runaway train. Visions of she and Fred together flashed through our minds as, at her invitation, we stumbled in and marched into the basement trying very hard not to fall down the stairs as we tried to look back over our shoulders at our hostess.

The games were started and we were soon joined by our friend who had arrived late and, judging from the look on his face, was in total shock and somewhat embarrassed.

"What's the matter?" one of our guys asked.

"I'll tell you later" he responded.

When Fred left the room to take care of something our friend said, "Let me tell you what happened."

"When I came to the door it was answered by this absolute vision. I know Fred and when I saw the person who turned out to be his wife I couldn't believe it and I said-: 'obviously, I'm at the wrong house but I'm looking for the Fred M. residence." Thank goodness the lady had a sense of humour because our man had just become a candidate for self-immolation.

It was a great evening and from that time on, we all looked at Fred a little differently and with a lot more admiration. But, this isn't the story I intended to tell you about the ping pong club.

Actually, I wanted to tell you about our plan to collect some money and to have a little get together after the ping pong season was over, whenever that happened to take place. We decided that we would each chip in twenty-five cents per week and save the funds for the big blow-out. We were really big thinkers and even bigger spenders.

The first bit of tension arose when someone missed a week but arranged for an alternate player. We had to deal with the question of whether the alternate was charged the twenty-five cents and, if so, was he to be included in the big blow-out or was the missing player to make up the assessment. I forget how that was resolved but it got a little hot.

The second bit of tension arose when the treasurer couldn't produce a proper report on how much we had collected to that point. I believe he resigned his post in disgrace.

The problem became over-whelming when we started to explore how and where the big blow-out would take place. Were we going out to a bar or restaurant? Were the wives included? What restaurant or bar? Why not go to a ballgame? Why not go to the race track?

The choices were endless and the arguments became more and more heated. The end of the ping pong season had come and gone. We were into lawn cutting, gardening, little league baseball and everything else that goes with summer. We would, however, meet at least every other week to try to resolve how and where we would spend the money we collected all year.

Friendships became strained. Coalitions of members would form and break up as the argument raged. Finally after almost two months of wrangling a solution was reached. We decided to just give the money to the humane Society and forget the entire deal.

It took a while to restore neighbourhood relations. We played ping pong for a couple of years longer. We were smart enough to just never collected any money again.

Optimist Attendance

I was never much of a joiner. I figured out that when you join something you eventually quit. As I didn't want to be a quitter, I avoided joining in the first place. To me, there was a convoluted logic in that approach to life that made sense. It also saved a lot of time.

When we bought our first house in Ancaster, which cost about half the price of my latest car, we were one more couple among many with no money. We all had common problems and we all fit into the same area of life. We also wanted to do the right things for our families, our communities and for ourselves. In order to do the right thing for the community, I was persuaded to join the Ancaster Optimist Club.

It was for men only but on Saturday mornings Wanda joined the other wives, known as Optimisses, (doesn't that curdle your porridge?) and made popcorn and supervised the Saturday morning movies for the kids. Most families only had one car so the movies shown at the highly mortgaged Optimist Hall was a big deal and the only game in town.

In order to pay down the mortgage and keep a central meeting hall going, the Optimist men would sell Christmas Trees, peanuts, light bulbs and run bingoes at the annual Ancaster Fair. Attendance at Optimist meeting was mandatory if you wanted to retain your good standing. If you missed three consecutive meetings you were drummed out of the club. If, however, you participated in any fund raisers or other Optimist endeavours, such participation counted as attendance at a meeting.

The first part of an Optimist Club meeting consisted of a happy hour during which most members, at that time, would get pleasantly swacked. We would then move to a short business meeting where we learned the results of the latest peanut drive, then a pleasant meal catered by the Optimisses. Then, a careful drive home.

There were those who loved the entire schtick and who wanted nothing more in life than to be elected the third vice-president of the Ancaster Optimist Club. There were those who liked the happy hour and the cheap drinks. There were those who just wanted to be out with the boys. There were those who wanted the good feeling that comes from helping out.

I was never that good at attending the regular meetings. I was in the construction business at the time and could always help out with a pick-up truck or some material needed for an Optimist project. That kept me a member in good standing and I could avoid some of the "bun throwing" meeting dinners. Wanda and I would attend the Christmas dance or bowl-a-thon. We had some fun and met people that we still know as acquaintances.

We had our dust-ups within the club. For example, there was a major battle over whether we played O Canada and God Save the Queen before meetings. To play both meant either cutting into the drinking time or letting the meal get colder. That was resolved by only playing O Canada and toasting the Queen. There was another major fuss when we discovered that the by-law of Optimist International precluded blacks from becoming founding members of new Optimist Club chapters. This was during the early 1960's and that kind of stuff needed to be changed. It was.

Every now and again there would be a very special Optimist Club event. The Great Grand Poobah from the district council was scheduled to come all the way from Buffalo to attend one of our meetings. He was to use the occasion to present perfect attendance pins to members of our club that qualified. It was to be a solemn, yet gala, event that ranked right up there with Oscar night.

Drinking was somewhat reduced that evening because we wanted to be on our best behaviour. We dispatched with the meal then waited as the Great Grand Poobah took the microphone. We were congratulated on building the hall. We were congratulated on reducing the mortgage while still raising extra money to send kids to camp. We were pleased to hear that our club was one of the fastest growing chapters in the district. Then we got to the really important stuff.

The Great Grand Poobah announced that we had no fewer than twelve members that qualified for the bronze lapel pin indicating one full year of perfect attendance at Optimist Club meetings. Led by Fred Adams through to George Young, we applauded them one and all, as they marched to the podium to collect their pin and receive a two-handed handshake from the Great Grand Poobah.

Next, it was announced that we had seven members that qualified for the silver pin signifying three years of perfect attendance. There was even louder applause and an occasional "bravo" was shouted.

Four members were then announced as having qualified for the gold lapel pin indicating five years of perfect attendance. The club members rose as one to applaud their commitment to community service. It was getting downright emotional and still the Great Grand Poobah held the mike.

When the members had settled back into their chairs and order restored to the room, the Great Grand Poobah announced that tonight was even more special because he had the proud task of delivering the gold lapel pin with diamond chip indicating ten years of perfect attendance. He informed us that there had only been thirty-seven such pins awarded in all of Canada and the continental United States over the past year.

Tonight, he announced that he had the privilege of delivering this unique pin to Optimist John Smith. "Unfortunately", he went on to say, "John Smith isn't here tonight …".

He went on to say more but I didn't hear it. Convulsive laughter somehow messes up my hearing. I was taken aside and told again how you could miss a meeting and still qualify for attendance. It was too late for me, however. I knew my career as an Ancaster Optimist was over. I knew I was in the wrong place with the wrong group when I saw that I was the only one that saw any humour in the fact that Optimist John Smith wasn't at the meeting convened to deliver his perfect attendance pin.

I resigned as an Ancaster Optimist a short time later. Under the circumstances, I never thought of myself as a quitter. It was more like Graucho Marx saying that he would never join a club that would have him as a member.

Negotiating

When Tammara was in grade thirteen the local High School teachers decided to go on strike. I gather there were issues that had built up for years but the strike was on. It became a real concern to parents with children that were in their senior year. Classes were not being taught. There was no certainty that exams would be given or marked. There was no way that the senior students could apply for places in Universities without marks. It was a mess.

I attended a meeting at the local High School that was intended to provide both the Board of Education and the teachers and the teachers union with some input from the parents. Views ranged everywhere from the position of "give the teachers whatever they want but get the schools re-opened" to "give the teachers nothing and let them walk around until they starve".

During my years in the construction business I had dealt with a number of unions and union issues. Our company had always worked with union personnel so I had some additional insight over many of the people affected by the strike. I had also long since concluded that strikes were usually ego trips, on both sides of the issues, and were among the dumbest ways to deal with things that I could possibly imagine. I still feel that way.

If I had been born in the coal fields of Pennsylvania in the eighteen hundreds and had been subjected to the "I don't care and in your face" management attitude that existed at that time, I would probably have been a member of the Molly McGuires and I could have been out there blowing up mining operations. However, this is not the eighteen hundreds and there must be a better way. I've also noticed that while strikes are in progress the so called leadership on both sides continue to live very well. Negotiations usually are moved to fine hotels where all parties live off expense accounts while the public, the shareholders or the strikers try to adjust their lives and make do.

I made the mistake of standing up and saying a few things at the meeting and the next thing I knew I was running for the School Board with the intention of becoming a contract negotiator if elected.

Several of my friends helped me out. We banged on doors. We gave away apples wrapped in "Vote for Me" papers. We shook all the hands we could find. We rode a horse and buggy around Ancaster with a "It's Time for Old Fashioned Values" message attached. We went to candidate public meetings. The meetings were the most fun.

There were a lot of ill feelings carried over after the strike and as a result, some of the meetings would get pretty hot and heavy. It was like old style stump politics. It was kind of fun. Following every meeting my wife would grab me by the sleeve and, before we even left the hall, she would be on my case about my slump style of sitting. I never really learned how to sit properly in a chair. I kind of camp. Wanda made sure that I knew I was a disgrace to the neighbourhood as far as sitting posture was concerned. My sitting in public style along with my selection of mix and match clothes have been the bane of her life.

I was elected anyways.

Through some internal politicking I got myself appointed to the Salary Negotiating Committee. After some pushing and shoving I was appointed Salary Chairman and that meant I would head up the negotiating team on behalf of the Board. A rather renowned Labour Lawyer had headed up the previous set of negotiations. He had a hard nose reputation and advised me not to enter into negotiations without a lawyer at the head of the team and to always be prepared to "take a strike". If you did get into a strike position he advised that you make sure you are prepared to keep the strikers out for a minimum of six weeks. He theorized that makes them feel the hurt and will reduce the likelihood of another early strike. It was indeed a hard nose attitude and it's amazing how many strikes last approximately six weeks before the parties get serious about negotiating a settlement. As I said earlier, strikes are primarily ego trips and they are really dumb most of the time. I also believe that any jerk can negotiate a strike.

We got lucky. The head negotiator for the teachers wanted to make a reasonable deal for all parties and get on with life. I felt the same. We were convinced by another Board member to try an approach called Single Team Bargaining. Instead of each side setting out their positions and trading offers and counter-offers back and forth, under Single Team Bargaining all sides put all the issues on the table at once and went problem solving. It was agreed that all the information, including budgets, would be put on the table and that no issue would be considered resolved until every issue was resolved.

The process involved a lot of trust and in an atmosphere that historically was always adversarial, trust didn't come easy. The teachers, the Board and the Administration all had separate agendas at the outset. It was difficult to forge a team approach among groups that never trusted each other and it took some time. The unusual approach, however, allowed us all to identify problems and design solutions that none of the groups could have possibly done on their own. We came up with a number of things that were far ahead of the times and that adversarial negotiating teams had never even considered but, make no mistake, it was not a love in but it was a system that was working.

As we were winding down to the end of the negotiations we knew we were getting close to an agreement and we knew we wanted the deal to work. We had all put too much into the endeavour to see it fail.

It was rather late at night and we had been in a negotiating meeting for several hours. Everyone was tired. Everyone was testy. I looked around the table and said,

"Everyone here is a little bit unhappy. The Administration is convinced they haven't got everything they want. The teachers feel the same and so does the Board. As everyone is just a little bit unhappy", I observed, "we're probably at the right place and we should have a deal."

It was a good observation and the deal was struck. Life is very much that way. I liked the way it was put together. The egos were parked and we all made a good deal.

I wonder whatever happened to that idea.

Captain Bean's Boat

I always wanted to visit Hawaii. I must have liked it because we eventually visited the islands four times.

Wanda and I made our first Hawaiian visit with another couple that we knew socially. We next visited Hawaii with Paul and Laura, sister-in-law and brother-in-law, on what was probably the most fun vacation for me, ever. Wanda and I took the kids out there during the Christmas holidays. The kids earned their air expenses by farm work and we covered their ground costs. A friend of mine and I went out there on a three day golf trip. He had earned some special air miles to be used within a specified time. A sixteen hour flight out followed by three golf games, then a sixteen hour flight back through several time zones left both of us very unsure over whether we were in Honolulu, Toronto or Zurich. It was nuts but it was fun.

Leading up to our first trip, Wanda and I were visiting with Alex and Joan and the subject of Hawaii came up as a vacation site. The next thing we knew, Alex had a fistful of brochures and we were booking flights. We arranged a three Island tour over a two week period. Alex suggested that, as we wouldn't be spending much time in the hotel rooms we should book moderate rather than superior accommodations. We went along with the idea.

Hawaii is as much an idea as it is a place. Our hotel in Honolulu certainly fit the moderate rather than superior category. It was clean, centrally located and in the midst of the idea of Hawaii. Our tour included a welcome breakfast. That turned out to be a three hour sales pitch for tours and other attractions. We were then bussed en masse to the absolutely, genuine and authentic Hawaiian shirt and muumuu factory. The men all bought at least two Hawaiian shirts that would never again see the light of day once we were off the islands. The ladies all bought at least two muumuus. Muumuus are the full length loose fitting dresses that are extremely colourful but that make sense on the islands. Hawaiian shirts, on the other hand, don't make sense anywhere.

That evening we had arranged to take in a Hawaiian dinner and while we were waiting in the hotel lobby we watched the idea that is Hawaii unfold. Men of all shapes, sizes and ages were lined up waiting for tour busses. They were all garbed in the wildest Hawaiian shirts you could ever imagine. Their ladies were waiting in their new muumuus wearing the Hawaiian flowers in their hair with the flowers, often orchids, behind the proper ear as suggested by the tour director. Flowered leis were hung around the necks of both men and women. The ladies, especially, were just aglow.

Everyone was a friend. It was like a giant costume party and everyone was delighted with it. It was also as if it was all a gigantic scam but that was okay because it was all so well done.

We avoided the tours, for the most part, and explored the island of Oahu by ourselves or with Alex and Joan. There is a solemnity about Pearl Harbour, with an oil slick still seeping from the over-turned battleship Arizona, that is very moving. It's easy to bring December 7th 1941 back to life. We snorkelled Hamuama Bay and saw what can be done in a marine reserve. We went to the requisite luau and ate poi. It does taste like wallpaper paste. We ate with chopsticks and sat with Al Lopaka in his little bar. He told us about being on tour with his band and waking up in "just another mainland city" and not even being sure of the name of the place. He is Hawaiian by birth and he said he decided then and there to stop bouncing around the world and to go home.

We rode an outrigger canoe off Waikiki Beach and had a person riding a surfboard pull alongside and take our pictures. We could meet him at a particular street corner and buy the snaps if we wished. He had a book of samples hung around his neck if you wanted to see his work. The entire sales pitch took place while he was riding a gentle wave back into the beach. He didn't even get his feet wet.

We were scheduled to visit Oahu, Maui and the big island of Hawaii. The worse part of the trip was the organized/disorganized transfers from one island to another. We were told to have our bags packed and outside our rooms for pick-up by seven in the morning and to have ourselves available for the airport bus by eight. The baggage was never picked up before nine. We were never picked up before ten-thirty. You sat around in travel clothes in a bus, airport, airplane or another bus on the next island until you were dropped off at the next hotel to await your baggage which was expected by approximately three-thirty. The situation caused me to become somewhat peckish.

For those who are not sure of the definition of peckish, I suggest you stand behind me in a cafeteria line in Hawaii at about three o'clock in the afternoon on a sunny day with a gentle breeze and an outside temperature of 75 degrees. Make sure I am wearing travel clothes that are too warm and that I had worn since seven in the morning. Then make sure that I haven't had anything to eat since eight o'clock in the morning. Then you should bang me in the small of my back several times with your tray in an effort to move me along at a pace that suits you. I will then let you know, very clearly, what peckish means.

A lady in a cafeteria in Maui tried exactly that and I told Wanda that if the lady bumped me one more time she is likely to get decked. The fact that the lady was in her eighties probably would not have saved her. Wanda, being a Libran diplomat, sent me to a table near the air conditioner and eventually brought me sustenance. She may have saved me a jail term.

Our hotel room on Maui, being of the moderate class, backed onto a parking lot but you could see the path to the beach. I didn't notice the dumpster until it was being emptied at six o'clock the next morning. Wanda and I agreed that as our moderate accommodations on Oahu gave us a great view of an apartment building and as this room gave us a great view of a parking lot, we would upgrade when we got to the big island of Hawaii. We may never pass this way again.

When we got to the island of Hawaii, sure enough, there was the parking lot and there was the dumpster. When asked, the room clerk offered us a beautiful room at the front of the hotel facing the ocean. It had a sit-out balcony that over-looked the beach, a boat dock and also over-looked the hotel outdoor entertainment area that would spring to life complete with hula dancers every evening. It also had a connecting room that could be made available to our travelling companions at a very nominal upgrade price.

We jumped at the deal but our friends declined because as they said, "you don't spend much time in your room." That evening, after dinner, they asked if they could take a look at our room.

"This is really nice", offered Alex.

"Oh, look at the lovely chairs and table on the balcony", observed Joan. "Do you mind if we sit out for a few minutes?" and made themselves very much at home.

There were only two balcony chairs and they suited Alex and Joan. Wanda and I sat out on two straight backed chairs we took out of the room. They accepted our offer of some refreshments and, while I went for ice, they settled in to enjoy the Hawaiian band and the hula dancers.

We watched as couples and groups started to gather at a boat docked at the pier below our balcony. The sign at the gathering place read, Captain Bean's Boat" and offered a three hour cruise, refreshments included. People were gathering very quietly. Introductions were being made and passengers were finding their way on board. As no one really knew what to expect it was a reserved crowd. Lines were cast off and away they went and disappeared into the warm tropical night.

We sat on the balcony and enjoyed the entertainment below. I think I needed to order more soft drinks and ice cubes but Alex and Joan were comfortable and Wanda and I found the straight backed chairs not too bad if you didn't try to lean back.

About three hours later we could hear singing on the Pacific. It wasn't very good singing but it was loud and well intended. It wasn't too unlike the singing we get in our office when someone brings in a birthday cake. Actually, it was bad singing. We could soon make out the running lights. It was Captain Bean's Boat, its passengers and its crew and it was a happy ship indeed. Whatever Captain Bean was serving, it sure seemed to work.

The best part of the evening was watching the passengers disembark.

There was some unsteadiness as they came down the gangplank but we put that down to sea-legs. It was great listening to this reserved group of strangers that were reluctantly shaking hands just a few hours earlier.

"If you're ever in Peoria, make sure you give us a call."

"Bring the grandkids next time you're in Atlanta. You can stay with us."

"I've never met a Canadian before in real life. You guys are great."

"My cousin Ned lives in Vancouver. Maybe you know him."

We were there for three nights and Captain Bean pulled off the same caper every night. We know this because the four of us sat on our balcony every evening after dinner and watched it happen. In the meantime we enjoyed the entertainment and the hula dancers right below our room.

Alex was right. They don't spend much time in their room.

Selling the Farm

Once I realized I was never going to be a professional hockey player or a big league baseball player I turned my mind to other goals. It seemed that one could have a great life if one wrote books and stories for a living and lived on a ranch.

With this as a goal, we bought a forty-eight acre farm on Jerseyville Road. This was not the type of spread that one saw when you turned on Bonanza on a Saturday night and checked out the Ponderosa. It was a pleasant acreage with rolling hills. It had an age old storage barn that looked like it could fall down. It had an age old storage shed that looked like it had already fallen down. It had a seventy year old insulbrick house that had collected more than its fair share of varmints over the years.

We had put together enough money for a downpayment and we had staked out a corner of the property for our new house. We were our own contractors on the house and I was able to buy certain materials and services at a reasonable cost through connections we had in the construction business. Dollars were scarce.

Even after finding every possible dollar and cutting every corner we came up short on the funds we needed to purchase the property and build the new house. We answered this problem by entering into a partnership with another couple. They agreed to live in the old house on the property and to take care of the boarding of some horses and helped out with other farm responsibilities. Their help and the revenue brought in from the rent and the horse boarding made the deal complicated but feasible.

Part of the deal required that we each keep an accounting of money that we spent on the property or for the upkeep of the farm. If the farm was ever sold, we would each recover the money we spent on the farm and any surplus would be split evenly. Conceptually and on paper, it worked. In actual fact it worked for quite some time but partnerships are difficult.

I don't know when or why it started to break down but at some point neither partner was very comfortable with the other. Both had the feeling that the other wasn't doing their fair share of the work or meeting their responsibility or whatever. We had three children that became a bother to them. They had no children at the time. A lot of things went off the rails.

It became apparent to me, that the partnership would not work and that a division of the farm was impossible. There was no option, in my mind, other than to sell the property, pay ourselves back our own investments and expenses, split the surplus, if any, and move along with life. The agreement contained all the provisions necessary to take those steps.

There was only one major problem. Our partners were quite content in their little old house and told us they had no intention of moving or selling. They also made it clear they had no funds available to buy out our share so that we could move on with our lives. It was like receiving a life sentence to a rock fight.

We felt there was no recourse but to apply to the courts and have them order a sale and an enforcement of the contract.

We made application and after almost two years of delay we finally received a court order that required the sale of the property at public auction. I had never had any good things happen to me at auctions. Those who have read about my experiences at the cattle auction will know what I mean.

We really liked the property. We liked the home we had built. The kids liked the horses. We liked the neighbours. The idea of selling something we had worked very hard to get in the first place was extremely difficult but you can't live with a feud.

We figured that we could re-mortgage our house and the entire property and come up with enough money to buy out the partners. This would leave them with money in their pockets and save us uprooting. They didn't like that idea either so the auction was on.

We put up with four weeks of prospective buyers wandering around the property and then a week of such people trucking through our home. The entire process made us even more determined to try to buy the property back at the auction and see the end of our partners.

I'm going to use fictitious numbers to illustrate what we were trying to do:

We felt the house and property would sell for approximately $200,000.

Our partners were entitled to half that amount less our expenses on the property over the years. They would receive $100,000 less the $40,000 we had invested in the downpayment and in the barns and buildings we had improved. They would, therefore, be entitled to $60,000 for their net share. I needed to come up with $60,000 for the partners plus another $75,000 to pay off the existing mortgage. I knew I could raise a mortgage of $135,000 and handle it. All I needed to do was buy the property for $200,000 or less and it would all work.

Keep in mind that this was all taking place in 1973 and $135,000 was a huge mortgage at that time but we were determined that we could handle it. Anything beyond a payout of $60,000 to the partners would need to be added to the mortgage amount and we could not afford to carry a larger amount.

The day of the auction arrived and we gathered in a Court House room along with several potential bidders. The bidding, to our surprise, was opened by our partners at $150,000. They had obviously found an angel that was bankrolling their cause. Someone raised the bid to $170,000. Our partners raised to $175,000. The other bidder went to $180,000 and our partners dropped out of the bidding. We then entered the bidding and raised the bid to $190,000. The other bidder then dropped out.

I thought, "We've pulled it off."

At that point, a different bidder jumped in and offered $195,000. I countered with $200,000 and knew then that we were tapped out. The new bidder, without any hesitation, said $210,000. Also, without any hesitation, I offered $220,000. Wanda, sitting beside me was having a fit and my shins were turning black and blue from the kicking I was getting under the table. The new bidder offered $230,000. I said $235,000. He said $240,000 and I lost my nerve. By that time Wanda was in a pale sweat and my shins were in ruins.

We congratulated the successful bidder and as soon as we were out of earshot, Wanda lit into me.

"What were you doing? We couldn't raise $205,000 never mind $235,000."

"I know that", I explained "but the other guy didn't, and we just made half of an extra $40,000. We can now buy the place down the road and start over but do it right."

The golfer Lee Trevino was once asked if playing in a major golf tournament really increased pressure. Trevino said, "Playing in the U.S. Open isn't pressure. Playing a big tough Texan for $20.00 with only $5.00 in your pocket, that's pressure."

I kind of felt some of that at the Court House auction and it took my shins a long time to heal.

Little Guys

Studies seem to indicate that people who are taller than average seem to do better, in our society, than most other people. As I've been painfully average in height and in most other areas of my life, I can only rely on studies for that kind of information. I do believe in "the little guy syndrome". This is described as the sometimes chippy air and demeanour that is often taken on by persons who are vertically challenged. In an effort to prove that height has nothing to do with ability, some such persons seem to feel the need to take on a strut or rooster walk bearing to the point where they become off putting even before they are introduced.

Napoleon, it is said, had an attitude. Anyone that would line up soldiers and shoot every tenth man "so as to encourage the rest", had an attitude. He also caused a lot of shuffling in line.

Two of the biggest men I ever met or had dealings with were in the 5'4" range when measured head to toe. Jim K. ran his own construction company. He started from scratch by going door to door during the depression years and doing contract roofing and house repair work. He claims that on a couple of occasions people refused to pay him for roof work done so he devised a very simple plan. When he completed a roofing job he would block the chimney. He would ask for his agreed upon payment and, if someone refused or tried to horse him around on the price, he would take his ladder and leave. He said it cost him a few dollars of time and some material occasionally, but he left content in the knowledge that the cheat would pay a much bigger price the next time the furnace was lit and the house filled with smoke.

If he was paid his agreed upon price he would go back up and remove the obstruction. He claimed he very seldom ever had to use the plan because most people are very honest. He just used it with people who tried to jerk him around. I believed him. I found you could do business with Jim based on a handshake. His word was stronger than any contract ever written.

Cancer got Jim before his time. He was an honest throwback to a time before cost controllers, bean counters, lawyers and accountants were put into place to complicate the most simple deals. Jim was gone before the U.S. elected a President that defended himself with those immortal words, "It all depends on what the definition of is, is." Jim would have disapproved.

I was no longer in the construction business when Jim died but made a point of attending his funeral and sharing stories with a lot of people who felt as I felt about him. I miss him.

Very early in my construction business career I was talking with Jim in his office. He had the biggest desk I had ever seen. He also drove the biggest car he could buy. These were probably the only two show pieces he used to offset the "little guy syndrome."

"Son", he said, "if you want to run your own business and succeed, I'll give you three pieces of advice. Take them to heart. One, be the first person in the office in the morning. Two, keep your hands out of the petty cash. Three, if you ever decide to fool around, do it in New York City." It's good advice on all three counts.

The other 5'4" giant that I came to admire was a tough little guy that ran the construction department at a large manufacturing plant. Most people called him Mr. F. A few people that knew him well called him "Pop". I always called him Mr. F. out of both respect and fear but we'll refer to him as "Pop" for the purposes of this story.

There is a culture in many industries, and it's certainly alive and well in the construction industry, to accept gifts, tickets to events and a lot of other niceties as "thank you" gestures. You did not do that with Pop.

I remember sitting in his office as he discussed an invoice he was expecting from a contractor that had done some painting at Pop's house. The contractor, apparently, suggested that they just forget about the bill. Pop told him, in no uncertain terms, that he wanted a full and proper invoice for the work. He wanted it that day and if the invoice was not on his desk by the end of the day, that contractor would never lift another paint brush in "his plant" again.

Pop would never, to my knowledge, accept or suggest anything for himself but he had another side. He had a soft spot for kids and particularly for kids with health problems. Almost single handed he organized, furnished and equipped a clinic for kids with a particularly debilitating disease. At one time or another, almost every contractor that worked in "his plant" had been touched by Pop for a donation towards this particular endeavour. We would get a call and it would go something like this-:

"Son, the centre needs a Van to transport some of the kids back and forth to their homes. A bunch of contractors are kicking in "X" number of dollars to get it bought. Are you interested in getting in on that deal?"

Of course the kids got their Van. Of course it was a form of coercion. Of course it probably wasn't the proper thing to do, but it felt right.

Pop was a member of the Shriners Club and they sold Christmas Cakes each year to raise funds for needy kids. Pop was always right in the thick of it. Every year, in early November, I would get a phone call from Pop.

"Hello son, it's Christmas cake time again and I marked you down as wanting 48 cakes. Do you have any problem with that?"

"No sir, Mr. F. In fact I was just sitting here wondering where I could buy some Christmas Cakes this year."

"Consider it done. Just drop your cheque off at the Shriners Club. Thanks."

A month would go past with no cakes. Then I would get another call.

"Hello son, remember those cakes you bought?"

"Yes sir, Mr. F. How are they doing?"

"The cakes are doing fine but I figured you'll never get rid of 48 cakes so I donated 36 of them to our Christmas basket program. Do you have any problem with that?"

"No sir, Mr. F. In fact I was just sitting here wondering how I could possibly get rid of all those cakes. Thanks Mr. F."

"No problem son. That was a generous gesture on your part."

Another two weeks would pass and we would get a third call.

"Hello son, remember those 36 cakes you donated to the needy family Christmas baskets?"

"Yes sir, Mr. F."

"Well, the baskets are put together along with lists of where they're supposed to go. I didn't think you would have any difficulty in getting your 36 delivered for us. Do you have any problem with that?"

"No sir Mr. F. In fact I was just sitting here wondering what I was going to do with all my spare time between now and Christmas."

"Thanks son, and son, Merry Christmas to you and your family."

And Merry Christmas to you Pop. Wherever you are. I've known some really big people in my life. Some of them were only 5'4".

Nuts

In 1944 the Allied armies were sweeping across Europe driving towards Germany and its Capitol Berlin. The war was thought, by many, to be virtually over as the German army was out of fight and rapidly running out of resources.

Suddenly, to the shock of the Allied Command, the German army regrouped and counter attacked through the Ardennes Forest catching the U.S. Army totally by surprise. A huge bulge was created in the Allied lines as they bent but didn't break before the German onslaught. The battle of the bulge was on.

The 101st Airborne Division, commanded by Anthony McAuliffe, found itself trapped and totally surrounded at a little town called Bastogne. There was no hope for any relief from Allied ground troops. Weather conditions prevented planes from flying so there was no hope for any relief from the skies.

The German commander, confident that the 101st Airborne was finished, sent a demand for surrender to Anthony McAuliffe. The German commander explained the predicament to McAuliffe and demanded a sign of surrender in order to prevent additional unnecessary bloodshed. McAuliffe reportedly responded with the single word, "nuts". There are those who believe the response was much more salty but the news media couldn't use some of the words that are now commonplace in our papers. "Nuts" was the quote.

The 101st held on until General Patton turned his army around and broke through the German lines to relieve McAuliffe and his men. The Division became known as "the battered bastards of Bastogne. McAuliffe became a general and a legend.

In 1956 my nephew Jim, having joined the U.S. army for whatever reasons, found himself in occupied Berlin as part of the Army Rail Transport Service. Jim had worked with the railroad in Canada before he joined the army so it was natural that he wind up in the rail service area. During World War II most cooks by trade wound up assigned to the transport section of the military and most electricians found themselves assigned as cooks. This is part of the process that cause people to believe that "military intelligence" is the perfect oxymoron. However, I digress.

Jim was in Berlin and between the time he spent touring the city, sampling German beer and courting his wife to be, Renate, he served as part of the rail transport service in the army. Berlin was under a four power occupation with U.S., British, French and Russian troops controlling the city in an uneasy truce. The Russians had designated East Berlin as theirs and made it clear they would tolerate no incursions of any type from any of their former allies.

The U.S. contingent had been informed to expect a visit from the legendary General McAuliffe for a troop inspection. He was to be accompanied by Mrs. McAuliffe and it was to be a spit and polish operation. There were to be no mistakes or the next posting would likely be Alaska in January.

Jim's group had been told that Mrs. McAullife's dog was being sent to Berlin via train. When asked why the dog wasn't flying in with the General and his wife, they were informed that the dog didn't like to fly. Who was to argue with General McAuliffe?

The dog arrived by rail, as expected and was given over to Jim for safe keeping until delivery to the general was arranged. Jim took some pity on the caged dog and let him out of the cage for water and a stretch.

As soon as the cage door was open the dog bolted. It went straight out the door of the transport depot and down the railway tracks towards East Berlin in the direction of the armed Russian and East German Volpo guards with Jim and his fellow soldiers in hot pursuit. A nearby Jeep full of MPs were also commandeered into action and the chase was on.

As they neared the East German border, the Jeep pulled up at the appearance of two armed and menacing Volpo guards. The dog, now exhausted from its run, decided to stop and lay down for a rest but not before it had crossed over into East Berlin. The guards had cocked their rifles.

Jim and his companions knew they now had to make one of two choices. One, they could cross into East Berlin risking an international incident and risking that the jumpy armed guards would start shooting at either them or the dog, or both. Two, they could give up on the chase, abandon the dog and face General McAuliffe.

It was an easy choice to make.

There was much smiling, waving, showing of empty hands, some bowing and generally behaving like frightened and cowered fools but Jim and his fellow transport soldiers advanced into East Berlin to recover the dog. It was obviously safer to confront two armed guards in East Berlin at the height of the Cold War than to explain an empty dog cage to General Anthony McAuliffe.

Fortunately for them and the dog, the armed guards lifted their rifles and let the recovery take place. Later that afternoon when the General's Aide came to pick up the dog and asked if there was any problem, the answer was "No Sir. Everything is A-OK."

Jim and Renate were married in Berlin. Patricia, their first of three daughters was born in Berlin. They returned to Canada and raised Patricia, Kim and Kelly. We see each other a little more now. It has been timely and it has been fun.

I still don't believe that General McAuliffe only said "Nuts".

Little Old Wine Maker

I first met Joe K. when he was a lawyer, fairly new to the profession, and we were in need of the services of a lawyer to incorporate a company. He had been referred to us by an accountant and we met in his office in the old Pigott Building in Hamilton.

His office was small with a little space for a secretary, yet to be hired, and enough room in his own office to hold his desk, chair, bookcase and a couple of small filing cabinets. His pictures and diplomas were spread around the floor. There were a number of boxes and small packing crates stacked in corners. From the look of the office, he had obviously just recently moved in. When I asked him how long he had been in that office space he replied, "just over two years".

He was a great guy. He had a face that looked like the map of Ireland and a laid back manner that left you feeling good about dealing with him. The look of his office after two years should have been a tip-off that he didn't always get to things as quickly as you might like but it was easy to like him and, eventually, he always got it done and it was done well.

Joe and I did a lot of things together and he was a good mentor. He was determined to become a lawyer but couldn't get into Osgoode Hall. He wound up getting his law degree from a University in New Brunswick. It may not have been as prestigious but Joe was a lawyer. He told me that if I ever became involved in a private company that I should take the office of Secretary. His rationale was that, as Corporate Secretary, you at least got to see everything that was done. It was good advice. I've used it and I've given it.

One might say that Joe was sometimes a little absent minded. I remember sitting in his office one day when he called his wife at home.

"Margaret, did I bring the car to-day?" he asked.

Upon being assured that he did he turned to me and said, "Now all I need to do is remember where I parked it." I think that was part of his "solve one problem at a time" programme.

On days when he did not bring the car to work he would take the bus from Ancaster to Hamilton. In the evenings, after a long day at the office, he would get on the bus at the Hamilton terminal and almost immediately fall asleep. He would be awakened by the driver when the bus reached Brantford and then buy another ticket back to Ancaster. At least he had grabbed a nap by that time and usually managed to get off the bus on the way back.

As time went along Joe became more and more respectable. Before he became totally respectable, he and I used to take a few minutes on an occasional Friday and stop off at a local watering hole to have a few pops. One night, time got a little away from us and I remembered that Wanda might be holding dinner for me. It was very close to 11.00 PM when I came to that realization.

I called her from the bar and said, "Why don't you go ahead and feed the kids. I might be running a little late."

It was not my finest hour and her response, which shall remain unrecorded in print, caused me to suggest to Joe that perhaps he should come home with me as I may need a lawyer.

His observation, after being met at my front door by Wanda, was that "this is the first time I ever saw Wanda look at you without the look in her eye being anything other than that of love." It was almost poetic. It may have saved a life or at least a marriage.

Joe was a city boy but, somehow, we convinced him to go fishing with us. Another Joe, a New Yorker who claimed he never wanted to go anywhere that wasn't paved, and a fishing friend and I were on the trip. We went to Lake Nipissing which was always famous for good pickerel fishing and is still famous for quick and violent storms. We set out one very calm morning with a very nervous city boy lawyer and a very nervous New Yorker. By the time we were about half way to our fishing destination we were well out into open water and the Lake was starting to go nuts. There was a sudden wind followed by sudden vicious white capped waves that were starting to roll over the sides of the boat.

My fishing friend and I were trying very hard to avoid causing any real concern for the other two. I had untied my shoes, in case I had to dump them in a hurry if we went over the side. I was operating the outboard motor while very intently watching the incoming waves and trying to slide the boat into them without shipping too much water. The New Yorker was looking around and enjoying the ride. He must have thought every day was supposed to be like this one. My fishing friend had a large bailing can and was quietly bailing water out of the boat almost as quickly as it came in. I was trying to pick a spot between waves that would allow me to turn the boat around without swamping, so that we could try to run with the waves and make our way back to the camp. We were in trouble.

Then we noticed lawyer Joe. Joe was a devout Catholic and he had picked up on the fact that we had some problems so he did what came naturally to him. He had his rosary in his hands and had gone straight to asking the Big Guy for some help.

My fishing and bailing can friend saw what was going on and said, "Joe, I'm getting tired. How about you bail for awhile and I'll pray." This suggestion was coming from an avowed atheist so I knew we were looking for help from all sources. We didn't drown, so maybe the Big Guy was listening.

Joe decided at one point in his life to make some homemade wine. He researched the project very carefully and was busily brewing his concoctions in his basement. One of the by-products of some wine making processes is the attraction that it has for fruit flies. Apparently Joe managed to attract much more than his share and the fruit flies had started to move from the basement to his main floor. His across the street neighbour would sit on his front porch and watch Joe through his dining room window. He could see Joe and his wife sitting at their dining room table enjoying their evening meal.

Suddenly Joe would lash out in all directions with either or both hands. There was clapping, clutching and even some ear swatting as Joe flailed away in all directions. The neighbour, having watched this pantomime for several evenings asked Margaret about it.

"Is Joe not well? I look through your window, trying not to spy, but it looks like Joe goes into some kind of arm swinging seizure every now and again."

"No" answered Margaret. "He's just making wine."

Joe died a judge but he died when he was too young. He was a good guy.

We Made a Video

A friend of mine once observed that his family must be dysfunctional in that they all seemed to like each other. He was right. Most families wind up feuding and fussing over enough minor things that they manage to cause major rifts at one time or another.

There are few things sadder than situations where a parent can't or won't talk to a child. It's even sadder when a child can't or won't talk to a parent. Siblings can't get together to celebrate a birthday because of something someone said to someone else ten years ago. Most times, we can't remember what was actually said by whom or to whom. We just know that we are still unhappy with each other and, therefore, can't get together just to talk.

My nephew, Jim, is twenty-one days older than me. His brother Mike was three years younger. They both spent as much time at our house during their childhood as they did at their own. They were brothers to me, more than they were nephews. From time to time, we would go long stretches without any real contact. We never seemed to have had any real falling out. We just went long stretches and never had contact. They went through the long light contact periods with each other as well. No one ever seemed to make the effort or have the time to find the other guy.

On those occasions when we did get together, it didn't seem long before we were re-telling the old childhood stories kid stories and enjoying them. Then, we would go away again.

We would remind each other of how Mike accidently rolled the car window up on the dog's neck and panicked. "What do I do now, Grandad? He yelled at my father.

"Roll the window down," came the laconic response. My father was a pretty basic guy.

My father's instruction to three little kids sitting in the back seat of the car during a country drive of, "don't you kids try eating any of those hot peppers we picked up" had no effect on Jim's decision to try one. His pleas to stop for a milk shake to help put out the ensuing fire had no effect on my father. He was not only a basic guy but he was pretty tough on occasion.

We would drift away from each other. We would drift back at a funeral or at a wedding. Like a lot of good people in a lot of good families, we wasted too much time away.

My friend Ted has a great fear of lightning. He especially wants absolutely nothing to do with being out on a golf course if there is any bad weather anywhere in the Province. Wanda and I were celebrating our fortieth wedding anniversary. Tammara was working out of town. Dan and Vickie had made plans to go away for the weekend. Linda was going camping.

We decided it would be nice to organize a golf game with Ted and Marianne and then have dinner with our two most longstanding friends. The four of us were together at our wedding forty years earlier so it only seemed right that we would spend a special anniversary in the company of each other. Especially, as Wanda and I were otherwise alone and feeling a little badly about it.

We teed off at 1:30 in the afternoon, expecting about a four hour round of golf and an early dinner. As we were nearing the halfway point in the round, I detected a very faint rumble of thunder in the very far distance. Knowing how Ted felt about such weather, I suggested that we should perhaps only play nine holes and go in. Ted, to my surprise said, "no lets play on. The weather will blow over."

It got a little darker and there were a few more distant rumblings. I again suggested that we cut the round short and go in. Ted, again, said he was fine with the weather and insisted that we continue playing. We played quickly, finished earlier than we expected and found ourselves back in the clubhouse just before five o'clock. We grabbed a shower then joined the ladies in the lounge area for a drink before dinner.

Ted seemed to be pre-occupied and much more quiet than his usual self. I asked if he was okay. He said he was fine but suggested that he and I go outside so that he could have a pipe. I was a little concerned about him and agreed, feeling that some air might do him some good. We spent a little time, he seemed to be somewhat relieved, then we returned to the lounge.

He and Marianne gave Wanda and I tickets for the Riverdance show and we were thrilled. We thought their offer to buy dinner was more than enough Anniversary present for us. We were getting ready to move to the dining area when the club hostess arrived and suggested, as this was a special occasion for us, that we have our picture taken so that it might be used in a club newsletter or some such thing.

We agreed and followed her upstairs. When we walked into the Main Hall upstairs, it was filled with forty years of our friends and neighbours. Larry kissed me on both cheeks. Wanda stood still and cried.

Linda, Dan and Tammara had put it together and it was a total shock. Ted's determination in keeping us out on the golf course and subsequently out of the room where our friends were gathering was nothing short of heroic. Andy had flown in from British Columbia. Jim and Mike and their wives, Renate and Marg were sitting together for the first time in several months. Alice had come down from Bracebridge. We saw some of the people that we had let drift for too long a time. The video that Linda had put together, after burglarizing our house for several weeks for old pictures, caused a lot of eyes to fill more than a little as a lot of people saw themselves as they touched our lives.

I warned Larry that he got away with being the only man to ever kiss me on both cheeks without my throwing a punch. It was everything we needed or wanted.

The spirit that put that party together continued after the balloons came down. Jim and Mike saw much more of each other than they had for years. Our family group made a point of making more contact. We had our own Oscar night and submitted home videos made for the occasion. Mike did Rocky in his film. Less than three years later, I got the phone call informing me that Mike had died. We were glad for the time and the contact that had been renewed through an extraordinary surprise party.

We made videos, showed them and laughed. We shared pieces of our lives with each other again, if ever so briefly. It happened because of a surprise anniversary party. Thanks guys.

Restaurants

Restaurants have given me way more trouble than I deserve.

Back in my "I'll do anything to get a job" days I worked at the Royal Connaught Hotel in Hamilton as a food storeroom helper. It was a good solid position and not "one of those up and down jobs" as my hiring boss described the elevator operators position. I eventually worked my way up to head stores person. There were only two of us. Then I became the Hotel Food and Beverage Controller. I held that job until the person that hired me had an unemployed relative and then out the door I went.

It was devastating at the time but it helped me determine that I would rather work for myself than depend on the whims of someone else. Especially when the someone else describes an elevator job as being "up and down".

When we were going through a particularly difficult time in our lives we called upon my experiences in the food business and started a catering business. It helped us at least have some cash flow and we ate our own food. It was a terribly difficult job and it went a long way towards developing a better understanding and tolerance towards those who work in the food industry.

Despite bringing all such additional tolerances into play, I still feel I too often get a bad time in restaurants and because of my additional tolerances, I still believe I get more trouble than I deserve.

When I go to an ordinary eating place I don't expect five star service. When I go to an advertised quality restaurant, I don't expect, nor do I tolerate, inferior food or inferior service. If the service and food is reasonable I usually over-tip. If the food is ordinary but the service is good, I still over-tip. It's seldom the food servers fault that the steak is tough or that the salad is wimpy.

My sympathy is usually with the food server. We were having dinner at a fancy club that was extremely busy at the time, when a customer demanded of a passing waitress, "Miss, get me some water."

As she was carrying two trays of food at the time she responded, "I'll be with you in a minute sir."

As she rushed past going back to the kitchen the client demanded even more loudly, "Miss I told you I want a drink of water."

"I'll be right there sir", she said.

As she flew back to the other table she was serving carrying another loaded tray, the even louder customer said, "Miss, I told you I want a drink of water."

She very quickly returned to his table and said, "would you like a glass of water or shall I bring a pitcher?"

His response was, "I don't drink out of a pitcher." Her response to that was "well, that surprises me." She probably lost her job because of the ensuing brouhaha, but I was on her side.

A group of us took a golf trip to North Carolina. It was one restaurant problem for me after another. All my pals could order and very quickly, without any hassle, get what they ordered and enjoy their meal.

Not me. It was one disaster after another. I just got testier every time we went into a place to eat and we hadn't even arrived at the location where we were spending the golf holiday.

We stopped for breakfast the first morning on the road. Eight men gave the waitress their orders. I was the eighth. The person that ordered just before me said "I want orange juice, coffee, bacon with two eggs over lightly and brown toast". It was dutifully noted by the waitress.

Knowing that things go awry for me in restaurants I kept it simple. "I'll have the same", I said.

When the breakfasts arrived everyone got what they had ordered except that I had no orange juice. "Miss, you forgot my orange juice". "You never ordered orange juice" she replied.

Up goes the blood pressure. "Miss, if I said I wanted the same as him" indicating my friend, "and he is drinking orange juice, how in hell could I have not ordered it?"

"I don't know. How am I supposed to know how you think" she sniffed.

Okay, so it was just one bad experience and we still have a lot of travelling to do, for lunch we stopped at a family style restaurant that had a fast and inexpensive lunch buffet. This is exactly what we were looking for when we're on the road trying to make time.

I took a few things from the buffet, ate a little salad and saved room for a soft ice cream cone that was part of the self-serve buffet. I've never been good with equipment. In fact the office staff refuses to allow me to re-fill the paper tray in the copying machine ever since the service man had to be told that no one had any idea how the tray got jammed in backwards.

The soft ice-cream dispenser involved positioning the cone and setting two levers, then holding the cone under the dispenser while pulling down on the release lever. That I could handle. However, as the cone filled, I discovered that I had not figured out the shut-off mechanism. The cone filled to the top. I tried pushing the lever to make it stop. The cone filled beyond the top. I tried pulling the lever to make it stop. I moved the cone lower to give me more build up space while I tried moving the lever to the left to make it stop. I moved the cone even lower while I tried to push the lever to the right to make it stop.

By this time, I had lowered the cone to close to floor level and had a soft ice-cream head above the cone of at least ten inches in height when the next person in line, watching what I was going through, reached over my shoulder and pushed the STOP button.

When I was making my way back to our table balancing a ten inch pile of ice cream on a three inch cone the restaurant manager, a know it all 17 year old, said to me, "Sir, you didn't need to do that. You can go back as many times as you want." Another great restaurant experience.

Dinner the next evening was more fun for me. Seven people of our party of eight ordered steaks. They delivered the steaks as they came off the grill. Finally, after a long wait I corralled the waitress and asked about my dinner that had not yet turned up.

"I'm sorry, sir," she said, "I must have given your steak to the fellow that ordered the chicken and forgot to put his order in." In other words,

Kenny had eaten my steak and I didn't even get to eat his chicken because the waitress had forgotten to order it.

As you might imagine, by this point I was a really happy guy both with the restaurant industry and with my golfing buddies who, by the way, were doing just fine.

My old pal Ted suggested that when we get to our destination we would eat out the first evening at the fanciest place around. He told me to order whatever I wanted and that he would order exactly the same thing so that, between the two of us, we could wind up with one meal that is absolutely flawless. I agreed that the idea should work and that it might save a life.

We ate that night in the fancy dining room at the club where we were playing golf. Ted explained the stress that the restaurant industry had placed me under and that she was to pay particular attention to what I order and "for heaven's sake, get it right."

I ordered a Caesar salad, roast lamb with mint jelly, baked potato with sour cream, no vegetables and "we'll discuss dessert later". Ted put in exactly the same order.

My dinner arrived. I was served first. The waitress stood back and asked, "Is everything satisfactory? "

"You forgot the mint jelly," I said.

Her response was probably the best restaurant line ever-: "I'll knee walk it in, sir".

It was a great dinner and a great trip.

Golf Membership

Golf clubs are great in that they give you the opportunity of forming friendships and relationships that often last through the years. Golf clubs are horrible in that they leave you watching the ebb and flow of person's lives over long periods of time. Ebb usually over-powers flow and that sometimes gets difficult.

There are almost as many reasons for joining a golf club as there are persons who choose to join. Some people actually join so that they can play golf. I think they are in the minority.

We moved to Ancaster in about 1960. We moved into a house with three mortgages and a live in mother. Both were difficult to handle from time to time. Our new home was very close to the Hamilton Golf & Country Club which is one of the more prestigious golf clubs in Canada. My golfing to that point consisted of sneaking onto a public course and playing from the third hole through the sixteenth hole in order to avoid the starter and the playing fees. How was I to know that a golf game should require the playing of eighteen holes. I'm still not convinced.

The person who I was working for at that time convinced me that I should apply for membership at the HG&CC. He felt it would be helpful with business connections and that I might even have some fun playing the game. There was no mention of receiving any help with the membership dues but the suggestion made sense and the mortgages, if not the live in mother, were being handled a little easier by then.

I applied and discovered that I could make arrangements to pay the initiation fees over a period of time. That made that workable. I went through the interview process and waiting period and was accepted as a member.

Right about that time the person I was working for called me into his office and declared that he had received some negative comments about my application for membership. I couldn't understand where the complaints might have come from or what they might be about. He explained that some persons that our company did construction work for had made the observation that "the hired help shouldn't play at the same places as their bosses".

I was stunned. I was stunned at the attitude. I was stunned at the fact that this person I was working with would give it any credence. I was stunned that I was considered "hired help" when all along I had considered myself to be a working partner in our business.

I asked how I was expected to handle the situation and was told that I was expected to withdraw my membership application. There is a line in a fun movie where someone is advised against trying to do harm to a very difficult person. The advice given is, "don't shoot Mungo, it only makes him mad." The suggestion made me mad.

I explained to my compatriot that as he had nothing to do with making my application or paying my initiation fees or dues that he, therefore, had little or nothing to say about what I do. He got very brave at that point and announced that he and I would not play at the same golf club and that was the end of it. I asked him where then, he intended to play because I'm a member at the HG&CC. It was a rocky start but we managed to work our way past it.

It is a great place to play golf and, as a club, it will hopefully work its way past some of the antiquated attitudes it currently drags around so that it can also be a great club.

Although golf can be fun it can take up an enormous amount of time. I reached a point in my life where I was operating a construction company, running a small hobby farm, maintaining some interest in politics, working at a marriage and trying to keep a hand in with the raising of three small children. There wasn't much time for golf so I transferred from playing member status to social member status. I realize that the term social member when applied to me is an oxymoron that ranks up there with military intelligence and civil servant. But that's what I was called.

In the early 1980's our business was in trouble and the bank and I had to agree to disagree. The bank took over the assets of the business and sold them for a pittance. As the asset sale didn't produce enough funds to cover loans and interest, the bank took over our farm and home and sold them off as well. We were broke, out of a home and out of a job.

Right about that time, we received our invoice for the Social Membership at the Golf Club. It wasn't all that much but we were running on a totally empty tank. I told Wanda we couldn't pay it and, even if we could, we couldn't use the club because we couldn't afford to go out for lunch or dinner anyway.

At difficult times people that you are close with will either rally or totally blow apart. Wanda told me that we would not give up the membership. She told me that we will pick ourselves up off the mat. She told me we would need things to hang onto. She told me we would find the money. We did. We stayed.

We couldn't afford the time or money to play golf or be social for a long time. Dan took the old man out and we played an occasional round at some little course or other because he too said, "Dad, sometime you'll want to do this again." He was right and I wish he and I could play a little more often just for father and son fun.

Dan and I are now both members at the HG&CC. Wanda is also one of the most active golfers out there, having taken the game up. Sometimes when I walk around and get caught up in the beauty of the course and its environment I remember how close we came to never again having the opportunity of taking the enjoyment that can be taken from such a place. Wanda and Dan were in the right place at the right time. Thank you.

I'm still a rebel and will always be a bit of an outsider at such a place. I know there are people out there that have the same attitude as I encountered way back when I first decided to join. I know there are people that are hanging on to the mores and customs that have been in trouble since 1930 and that may eventually be dragged kicking and screaming into the 1950's. I tweak the odd nose and burst the odd bubble of pomposity. I don't like seeing young men that I knew in 1963 grow into old men and bend and eventually get honoured by a flag at half staff, but I'll hang around a little longer and see what happens.

The Runt of the Litter

I was the youngest of four children and, according to my mother, by far the smallest at birth. This story about the Runt of the Litter is not about me. It's about Sean.

For as long as I remember, we had a dog. In my earliest days it was Jerry, a wire-haired Terrier that actually belonged to my sister Alice but I kind of adopted him. Our next dog was a Boston Bulldog that I also named Jerry. I had a great imagination when it came to names.

Jerry was really my dog. He and I went everywhere and did almost everything together. I used to put a cardboard box in my bicycle carrier. Jerry would sit in the box as we travelled about, taking in the sights and making friends. He would sit patiently in the carrier box when I went into a store or did some visiting. He sat in the ballpark when we played ball. He was a boy's companion.

Jerry graduated to my first car which was a green 1947 Monarch Sedan. We were something, Jerry and I, as we travelled about. I remember having one of my many car emergencies, that came with the ownership of a 1947 Monarch, and leaving Jerry in the car at the garage while repairs were being made and while I went across the street for lunch. When I came back to pick up the car it was being circled rather warily by two mechanics trying to figure out how to get in to pop the hood and work on the repairs. Jerry, showing a territorial imperative that I had never seen, was bouncing from door to door making sure that no one got into "our" car. It cost me an extra hour of waiting but there was no mistake about whose side he was on.

He was a great friend but his day came. I cried that day.

Time moved along and while living in town in Ancaster, we bought a farm property and decided to build a house and live in the country. There was already a house on the property that we rented out while our house plans were put together. We decided that because we were moving to the country and would be in a somewhat more isolated situation that we should purchase another dog. We decided on a larger dog because it might have some intimidation value. As we had three small children we wanted a gentle breed that would be good around youngsters. We decided to get an Irish Setter.

When we went dog shopping we found an Irish Setter breeder that had four pups left. Irish Setter pups are all ears and all paws. The four pups were absolutely delighted that someone had come to visit them. Tongues were flying and tails were wagging everywhere. There was one little guy that, try as he may, couldn't quite get into the forefront of the greeting parade. His larger siblings made sure they pushed him back and made sure they were first in line. His tail was wagging just as hard as all the others but he was just pushed out of the way. We took him home and named him Sean, a good honest Irish name.

Sean grew into his ears and paws very quickly. He had that beautiful deep red coat, highlighted just a little with a deep rust. He had a great temperament and loved greeted everyone as if they were a long lost friend. My family claimed he was just a little cross-eyed but I never wanted to notice. He had a devil may care attitude that I used to refer to as his "Charlie Potatoes" frame of mind. You could watch him as his mind worked through things and he concluded, if I do such and such, I'll be in trouble but what the heck. It looks like fun.

Sean was kept outside in a sizeable pen with a well insulated dog house. There were many days when he lived as well or better than I did. We finally received permission to build our house in the country and started construction. We still lived in Ancaster while the house was being built.

Once the house was started we noticed that construction materials and supplies were being stolen from time to time. I asked the people renting the house at the back to keep an eye on things but they never saw anything go missing. There was no problem during the day because either Wanda or myself were around often enough to deter thieves but the place was being hit at night. Construction had reached the stage where we had fixtures and other costly items in the house that we just didn't want to lose.

We decided, that as construction had reached the point where we had electricity and telephones, I could spend the nights in the unfinished house and perhaps put a stop to the pilfering. We decided I would sleep in an upstairs bedroom and that I would take Sean with me for companionship and protection. I had strung out some empty tin cans on wires around the house positioned so that an intruder would probably bump the wires and set off a warning noise. I settled into my rented cot with my back to a recently installed window with Sean lying on the floor beside me.

At that time Jerseyville Road was still an unpaved dirt road. Any time you heard or saw more than two cars in any one hour, you had the feeling that someone was holding a parade without a permit. It was quiet. The countryside at night is black and is quiet. You don't hear road noises. You don't hear neighbours. You don't hear horns or sirens.

If you listen very carefully, you hear breezes rustling trees. They can sound like quiet footsteps making their way through the grass. If you listen very carefully, you might hear an occasional animal that might accidentally brush against a wire that has a tin can tied to it. It's scary. Both Sean and I were very aware of everything.

I thought I had heard a tin can noise. So did Sean. I was now sitting straight up in my cot pretending I was reading a Time magazine. I knew I was listening and not reading when I realized I had been on the same page for twenty minutes and that the magazine was upside down. Sean was on full alert and watching me.

All of a sudden, without any warning whatsoever, the window behind me came crashing down. I went straight up into the air, proving that levitation is a learned skill, and Sean went straight up with me. It seems that the window hadn't been properly adjusted by the installers and when the evening cooled down, down crashed the window.

Sean and I developed a very special bond having survived that incident together. He had a great life. We would go for a walk with me being determined that I could get him to follow without a leash. Sean would do that for a while and then he would wander a few yards away. He would come back when I called him. Then he would gradually wander a few more yards away and come back when called. I was pretty fast then and Sean, I think, had it figured out that with a headstart of less than fifteen yards, I could run him down and catch him. However, as soon as he had widened the space to sixteen yards he went deaf and couldn't hear his name no matter how hard I yelled and he knew the extra yard gave him his getaway room. We would get a call from people in Lynden or some other neighbouring village within a couple of days.

"We've got a Setter here with your name and phone number on a tag. He's just hanging around the house. We've been feeding him and he's fine."

I would go and pick him up. He would be delighted to see me and come bouncing over with his tail wagging and jump into the car where he would sit very proudly in the front seat taking in the sights. Every now and again I would get a nuzzle on the arm as he determined that things were still all right between us. He knew he was in trouble. He knew he would be spending more time on a leash. He knew I would be into more training sessions with him but the "Charlie Potatoes" attitude always won out.

He was a great friend, but his day came. I cried a lot that day. I still swallow hard whenever I hear the words in the song, "Mister Bojangles".

Dublin Airport

Peter O'Toole was a guest on a television talk show and told the story about his efforts to get out of Dublin Airport in a rental car. It seems that O'Toole was a notoriously bad driver and had never been able to obtain a drivers licence in Ireland. He had moved to the U.S. as a young actor and his success put him in chauffeured limousines so he had never obtained a drivers licence in America either.

He wanted to visit his native Ireland and he wanted the convenience of his own car so he arranged an international drivers licence that was much easier to obtain. He was required to take some lessons and learned to drive on an automatic U.S. manufactured automobile. When he got to Dublin Airport he discovered that the rental car was a standard shift and, of course, had the steering wheel on the opposite side of the car as, in Ireland, they drive on the opposite side of the road. He was in a panic but set off.

He claims that when he stopped at the first light, which comes up very quickly as you come out of Dublin Airport, he was waiting for the light to turn from red to green with a large truck in line behind him. The light turned green. The trucker beeped his horn. Anxious to get away from the light, O'Toole let the clutch out too quickly and stalled the car. Before he got it re-started the light had turned back to red.

When the light next turned green he was in an even greater panic and again stalled his car and again missed the light. At this point, the trucker waiting behind him climbed down from his rig and ambled towards O'Toole. A concerned O'Toole, was busy locking his doors and rolling up his window. The trucker leaned down and said to O'Toole, through the rolled up window, "Is it a particular shade of green that you'd be waiting for sir?"

When we visited Ireland we scheduled the first three days of our trip to be spent in Dublin. We did as much as we could during those three days and left with the feeling that we had merely scratched the surface. We picked up all kinds of brochures, maps, illustrations and all the paraphernalia that tourists collect. We had been advised to not drive in Dublin and we took that advice. We did arrange for a rental car to be picked up on the Sunday at Dublin Airport so that we could do some country touring at our own pace. While in Dublin, we travelled by bus most of the time. That was fun and it gave us an extra exposure to the friendliness for which Ireland is famous and confirmed the belief that if you stop by an Irishman for long, you will hear a story.

We were waiting at a bus stop one morning and a little old Irishman asked us how we were enjoying our visit. We expressed our concern that you never knew what to wear when you go out because the nicest day could turn into rain very quickly.

He said, "I'll give you a hint about the Irish weather. When you're in Dublin and you can see the mountains, it means it's going to rain. If you can't see the mountains, it means it's raining already."

At any rate, on Sunday morning we caught the bus to the airport and made our way to the rental car location. I knew I would have my hands full, driving under Irish conditions so I was at least smart enough to arrange for an automatic shift as I wanted no part of a standard shift that had to be manipulated with the left hand.

We asked for, and received, directions out of the airport and to the road that takes you to the City of Cork. We were told to go to the round-about and pick up the exit to highway #12 and to follow that road until you come to a large Guinness sign and then take a left past the Church and then watch for the sign that tells you that you need to turn left to get to the road to Cork.

"You can't miss it", we're told. I've never found anything that I've been told "I can't miss". The Guinness sign was no exception this day.

If you're anything like me, you never listen past the first turn when you ask for directions but my wife and navigator is usually very helpful under such circumstances and I left the car rental counter confident in her ability to help me through any confusion.

It was a cold morning with a very brisk breeze. We found our car and set out to clear the airport. Our bags were in the trunk and our overnight stuff, along with all the maps, brochures and other collected information was tossed into the back seat. When we got to the parking lot check out area, I was still trying to figure out the workings of the power windows and trying to locate the signals and windshield wiper buttons and toggles. I very quickly figured out that all such items were the reverse of those we would find in a Canadian car.

I managed to find the button that lowered the window on the driver's side so that I could turn in our airport pass. Then I couldn't figure out how to get the window back up. I also learned that when I reached for the lever that would be used to signal a turn I, by location habit, turned on the windshield wipers. While I was trying to figure all of this stuff out we arrived at the described roundabout. This had come upon us much more quickly than I expected and before I had the chance to even drop a prayer to St. Patrick, I was in a round-about posted for 30 kms per hour, travelling at 50 kms per hour with a Dublin driver on my bumper wanting to travel at 70 kms per hour.

"Roll up your window, it's freezing in here", Wanda demanded.

I hit a button I came into contact with and managed to roll down the window on the passenger side.

"Up, not down" I hear.

By this time, I'm halfway around the roundabout and I've got a lot more on my mind than figuring out windows go up or down. I know I need to move to the outside of the roundabout so I reach for the signal lever and flip it up. It immediately turn on the windshield wipers.

My mind was now in panic mode. "Okay" I think, "Switch lanes anyways and bail out at the next exit and we'll figure it out from there."

Now I find myself on a highway that is posted at 90 kms per hour with me going 110 kms per hour and the Dublin driver on my bumper wanting to go at 130 kms per hour. I'm also now trying to figure out which is the fast lane and which is the passing lane so that I can drive in a slow lane, if there is such a thing.

"Please, get the windows up" I hear from Wanda. She had passed through panic mode and had switched to whining and pleading. This is just one step short of tears.

I hit another button and manage to roll down one of the back windows. This, in turn, creates a major wind tunnel throughout the car and this sets every map, brochure and illustration that we had dumped in the back seat into motion and flying wildly around our heads.

"Get the windows up, you turkey" I hear "and get over into the slow lane". At least she had skipped past tears and had gone to straightforward anger.

I try another button and manage to get the fourth window down. By doing that I increase the intensity of our wind tunnel and there is paper debris everywhere. I figure out where the slow lane should be and flip on the signal arm and cut sharply towards the right lane.

"Watch it", she yells. "You cut that guy off and almost got us all killed. What's the matter with you?"

"The S.O.B. should have known I was making a lane shift," I answered. "He should have known I'm a tourist and he must have seen that I had my windshield wipers on".

We never did see the Guinness sign. We took another three hours to find the road to Cork. It was a quiet drive indeed. We did agree, however, that I would never again drive in Dublin.

Peter O'Toole thought he had problems.

Dancing I- Netting Pickerel

Dancing, as it is generally defined involves the movement of feet and other body parts to the sound of music. I have always hated dancing as defined in the foregoing. I met Wanda at a dance but that was just good luck and I was under duress having recently attained the ripe old age of nineteen and having recently given up on girls as not being anywhere near as reliable as the fun one could have playing baseball.

I generally get stuck going to one or two events a year and having what is affectionately referred to as "my annual dance" with my wife and occasionally with some other lady. Don't get me wrong. I really like ladies and their company but I find dancing a threat of some kind. Perhaps, it's as simple as not wanting to do things that you are not very good at, but that would eliminate almost everything for most of us.

I once chose to go to the lakefront during Hurricane Hazel and fill sandbags as a volunteer during the height of the storm rather than go to a dance that I was scheduled to attend that night. I found, much to my amazement, that my friends considered me to be somewhat of a hero because of my selfless acts that night. I just wanted to get out of going to the dance and working in the teeth of a hurricane was much more preferable and a hell of a lot more fun.

I've found a great need for another type of figurative dancing. All too often I say or do things that start to get me into trouble. At times like that, I often recognize that what I am doing or where I am going or what I am saying, can only turn out badly for me.

So we turn to verbal dancing. This involves recognition of the situation, a sense of humour or sense of the ridiculous, a bit of the way with words and sometime a touch of luck.

For example, three friends and myself were on a little fishing trip. We spent most of the fishing time still fishing out of the same boat. At that time there was still an abundance of fish in Lake Nipissing and the fishing would sometimes get very active.

As there were four of us in the boat, we each took turns netting the fish for a partner. This enabled the person with the fish on line to concentrate on getting it to the boat while another person made sure it was properly netted. Russ and I were partners on a particular fishing evening.

We went through a spell where we were both hooking a fair number of fish. It seemed that every time Russ got a fish on, I would have the net properly positioned and very adroitly would land everything he brought alongside the boat. On the other hand, it appeared to me that every time I got a fish hooked, Russ was late getting the net into the water or had it in the wrong position, or had it jammed under the seat or was standing on it. At any rate, I was getting more and more testy over the fact that he couldn't or wouldn't properly land my fish and I let him know that by body language supported by an occasional caustic comment.

Things were getting more than a little tense in the boat and the so called "jolly good natured banter" had long since ended.

I got another hit and it felt like a good sized pickerel. When I got it up close to the boat I saw that it was a very good sized pickerel. I noticed that Russ had stopped fishing and had long since very carefully positioned the net ready at his feet. I realized that he had become very unhappy with me and with my stupid attitude. I knew I was in trouble and I knew the trip, that still had three days to go, was in trouble.

At any rate, I brought the fish alongside the boat and watched as Russ took the net, carefully leaned over the side, carefully lined up the fish, carefully slid the net into the water, and missed it. I then watched the man go to pieces.

He flogged frantically at the fish a second time and missed. He swung the net around to the back of the fish and missed it. He dipped the net below the fish and scooped upwards and missed it. He then tried something else with the net that I couldn't figure out at all and managed to get the hook, the fish and the net all wound together in a way that the entire mess was enmeshed with the fish hanging outside the net but tangled up in such a way that we could drag it aboard.

Everyone, other than poor Russ, was hysterical watching the performance. I then announced that what I had seen was absolutely the worse landing anywhere since the Hindenberg. It wasn't much of a line and it would have been lost on anyone who had not seen the great German Zeppelin by that name, crash and burn while trying to land in New Jersey.

It may, however, have saved the trip. Russ told us later that he had positioned himself to make one swoop at my next fish, pull it aboard and hit me over the head with it. I believed it because I saw it coming. Fast words and good luck. That's called dancing by my definition.

Thank God the fish was suicidal.

Dancing II- Slow Golf

Verbal dancing can be a life saving device. If it's done well it can sometimes help avoid personal injury. We all use it from time to time. Some never recognize it as the art form it can become.

Slow golf makes me crazy. I can miss a four foot putt if I walk up to it and hit it. If I walk around all sides of the putt and plumb bob it, then measure the wind velocity, then check the break of the green from at least six sides, then check the way the grain of the grass is growing, then check the time of day as that might have some effect on the dew point, the entire process can add a good three minutes to the shot. Then I miss the putt.

Most golfers I know or play with feel the same way. There are some that follow the process described above and still take 85 shots, on a good day, to complete their round. This approach to the game may help the ego by saving an occasional shot but it also results in five hour golf rounds. That makes for a long day and cuts seriously into the time that could be spent at the 19th hole enjoying a "pop".

It may not be quite that bad, but on a warm day it sure feels like it.

There is an excellent golfer who plays at our course and who has the reputation of being one of the world's slowest players. Every effort is usually made to avoid being caught behind this gentleman on any given Saturday morning. He is a very soft spoken, nice man who has quietly worked away at his golf game and at his law practice and has done well at both.

One Saturday morning my three pals and myself were out for our usual game. We managed to get off the first tee just before the gentleman described earlier. The course was very crowded and, therefore, the play was inordinately slow. We weren't really concerned because we knew that, although we had to wait on the group ahead of us, the group behind us contained our slow playing lawyer and would probably soon be well out of our sight.

Unfortunately, the play was so slow that while we were waiting to tee off on the fourth hole, the group behind us caught up. It was time for small talk.

"It's really slow out here today", said our lawyer friend.

"It must be" said I with my mouth running far ahead of my brain. "This is probably the first time in forty years that you ever caught up to someone on a golf course." I said it with a smile.

"I think I'll punch you on the nose" said our slow playing friend. He was not smiling.

At this point there was a rush of wind caused by my three pals disappearing under the bench and into the bushes. "Take cover, duck and run", was the message.

I figured it was time to start dancing.

"That's a thought that might well cross your mind in view of my loutish remark" I suggested, "but then, you would need the name of a good lawyer to defend the assault charge" still smiling.

"That's also a good thought", said my lawyer friend "but I probably couldn't afford me" he said.

Good verbal dancing on both our parts. As we hit off the tee and started down the fairway after our shots, one of my friends, having emerged from under the bushes asked me, "why in hell do you need to say everything that pops into your head?"

"He doesn't, thank God," proffered another friend, "or none of us could ever be around him".

Now, I thought that was kind of a compliment. I guess you need to think that way if you need to know a lot of verbal dancing steps and when to start. But then again, if I could get my mouth to work just a little slower than my brain I wouldn't get into these messes in the first place.

Dancing III-Bad Olympic Landing

My friend Andy lives on Vancouver Island. Several years ago he moved to the city of Vancouver from Fort Erie. After a time, I got a card from Andy that said, "My family has found me. Must move further west." He now lives on Vancouver Island, with his wife Shirley, where he seems quite comfortable with his model trains and some fishing.

We see each other a couple of times each year and he sends an occasional B.C. Salmon our way through his daughter. Andy and I only knew each other casually having been introduced by a mutual friend. When we lived on our farm his daughter Michelle had a horse that was boarded in Fort Erie and that had got into some health problems. We were able to be helpful to the horse and, as a result of that and some fishing trips, Andy and I have become good friends.

Our daughter Tammara was the one that did the work with the horse. Andy, a former teacher who left that profession because he didn't like the politics of it all, tutored Tammara in calculus in reciprocation so everyone won, including the horse.

Andy is a person of strong principles and even stronger opinions. Because he is often a reasonable man, I value his friendship very highly. I have concluded that if your opinion differs from his you would be well advised to either change your opinion or defend it with great tenacity. Andy will accept your defence as an intellectual challenge, at least until you have seen the error of your ways and accept his point of view. Much like myself.

We call each other from time to time. Most times the purpose of the call is to pass along a joke or an anecdote. Sometimes, we discuss a little business or the state of the world. Sometimes, one or the other simply needs to make or receive such a call. Sometimes, it's just good to hear the voice of a friend. As I've gotten older I've tried to make such calls to friends a little more often.

Andy likes my jokes and has been a great audience. He passes them along and, I'm sure, never gives me any credit but if his west coast friends think he's a wit and a good source of material, who am I to spoil their illusions.

I had called him one Friday evening to pass along a couple of stories and to lay on a few clever bon mots. The conversation moved on to other things and Andy started to tell me about how he was all upset over yet another infringement on individual rights. It seems that since the World Trade Centre terrorist attacks, airlines flying in and out of Salt Lake City, the site of the Olympics, had established a rule that all passengers must remain buckled in their seats for the twenty minutes after take-off and for the twenty minutes prior to landing. Apparently, some passenger had objected to the policy, had got out of his seat and into a confrontation with the aircraft staff. He was subsequently handcuffed and arrested upon landing.

Andy thought the rules and the treatment of the passenger were outrageous.

I said I felt that, under the circumstances, the rules were reasonable and the passenger behaved like a jerk.

Andy said it was outrageous. I said the passenger behaved like a jerk. We re-phrased, but then said the same things again. The temperature was rising.

Then Andy, as if trying to explain a complicated calculus problem to a child, asked me in a very condescending way, "What if you needed to take a poop? Do you think you should be made to raise your hand and ask permission to use the toilet?"

I said that, under the circumstances, that would probably be an appropriate way to handle the situation.

Andy switched from a condescending tone to a downright exasperated tone. "For God's sake, Pat, what if she said no. Are you expected to sit there and poop your pants?"

There was a major increase in temperature. I decided to dance.

"Gee Andy", I replied, "I've pooped my pants during all kinds of landings over the years."

"Good move", said Andy. "Man, you're a hard guy to hit." he laughed.

He's coming this way for a visit in a short while. We're getting together for a corned beef sandwich. We'll tell each other some lies and argue over who pays the bill.

Word dancing may be dangerous but it's fun.

The Wall

I worked with a person who was a U.S. citizen and who had a son at draft age while the Viet Nam war was in full swing. He taught me a lot about how people's minds work.

Before his son was accepted into a U.S. University that provided him with an exemption from the draft, he was a full blown dove who wanted the war to be ended immediately. Once his son was accepted and received the full draft exemption, he almost immediately became a full blown hawk and was prepared to see other sons sent to Viet Nam rather than seeing U.S. policy suffer. As the war intensified, the draft exemption for college students was rescinded. My friend immediately became a dove again and wanted all the boys brought home.

The attitude may not have been admirable but it was understandable. Unfortunately, it underscores the age old observation that old men seem all too willing to send young men out to die.

We in Canada, have been fortunate to have avoided most of the killing frays since World War II ended. We lost people in Korea. We lost people in various parts of the world on peace keeping missions. We continue to lose people in the name of dying for a cause. Suicide bombers wander the world convinced that they are right.

World War II had to be fought. Sometimes really difficult things need to be done but it's amazing how attitudes change when it gets too close to home. My friend with the draft age son taught me that lesson, not that it needed to be taught. The screwballs of the world need to be brought into line from time to time. It's just so unfortunate that there seems to be a never ending supply of such people and that the cost of stopping them is so high.

Viet Nam was brought starkly into focus every time you turned on the evening news. It was fought in our living rooms. Hopefully, it brought things home to a degree that we are determined to do everything possible to avoid having it happen again. President Truman's dropping of the A-bomb made a point that has kept even marginally sane persons from using such weapons ever since. The A-bomb probably saved more lives than it cost but it made the other important point. Don't do it again.

Viet Nam will eventually become a footnote in history. The names etched into the Wall will live much longer than their cause. They also form an almost perfect picture of the mix of people who died in that war. They are etched into the Wall in the order in which they died. There is no consideration of rank or position. There is no evidence of race or religion. There is just name after name after name after name. It's an awesome reminder of why we don't want to do certain things if they can, in any way, be avoided. If they can't be avoided, then remember the cost.

I've always been a big believer in knowing the colour of the sweater you're wearing and the name of your team. Loyalty to those on your side has always been a big letter word with me.

An association of Viet Nam veterans constructed a replica of the Washington memorial Wall and were visiting various cities with it. They set up in Confederation Park. Linda and I went out to visit. The people with the exhibit had advised that those who have strong feelings about that war not visit the Wall alone as it evokes very strong emotions. It was good advice.

The exhibit gave people in various areas of the country that would be unlikely to make a visit to Washington, an opportunity to see the replica and to pay their respects. That was taking place. Flowers, letters from loved ones, an occasional beer that you hadn't had the opportunity of having with your buddy were left at the foot of the Wall with quiet regard and regret. The motto of the Viet Nam veterans who were responsible for the exhibit was "Forget the War and Remember the Warriors".

I use it sometimes to work past the venality of a few and to appreciate the strength that flows from the efforts of basically good people. Personally, it has helped me as I've made decisions about the Catholic Church. It's a motto that can be used in any number of situations where we tend to get caught up in the wrong areas.

I did get to visit the Wall in Washington. Wanda and I arranged a trip so that we stayed just outside Washington on a Saturday night. The whole purpose of the stop was to be in a position to get into Washington on an early Sunday morning and visit the Wall before the area became overcrowded. I wore my sunglasses even though it was not a sunny morning. It's a sight that makes you ache. The persons that were there early that morning were not tourists. Most, seemed to have friends on the Wall. They weren't any more successful in hiding their emotions than I was with my dark sunglasses on. It's a difficult place to visit.

From time to time, when I'm trying to understand things beyond my ken, I go back to the idea of looking through the things you may disagree with and seeing the things that really matter.

It shouldn't take a war and thousands of names on a memorial wall to make us feel that way.

Oi Do Indeed

An Irish person will seldom use one word where two words will do. This trait is reflected in the Irish accent. We say "I". It's a simple one letter word. To indicate the singular, the Irish take a four letter word such as "coin" and drop the first and last letters so that "oi", as part of "coin" sounds like what we would say for the sound of "I". I could have told you that by just saying, the phrase "Oi do indeed" means the phrase "I do indeed" but that would have only taken one short line and would have been un-Irish.

Every time I thought about visiting Ireland, the Irish would do something stupid to each other and I would talk myself out of making the visit. We finally decided that it would be most appropriate to spend my sixty-fifth birthday in Ireland and so we did. It was a great trip. It was part "roots". It was part history. It was a lot of nostalgia. It was a lot of fun.

We did some tourist things but we stayed away from crowds and castles and concentrated more on the feeling and the history of the country and took from that a better understanding of whatever some of us find to be Irish in ourselves. I even discovered that I could like the taste of Guinness.

We rented a car so we could poke around at our own pace. We chose to stay at Bed and Breakfast places rather than hotels. We would recommend that to anyone making a visit to Ireland. We spent more time walking beautiful but desolate beaches out on the Dingle Peninsula than we did joining the tours that promise "a look at authentic Ireland". They were good choices.

We found that once people discover that you are going to visit Ireland, you are deluged with suggestions about where you must go and what you must see. It's well meaning advice but, if you took it all, you would need to stay in Ireland for several years. Once you have arrived in Ireland you are beset with another round of "must see" and "must do" items from the locals. Obviously, it means that there are all kinds of "must see" and "must do" things in that country.

We saw the country we wanted to see. I would have liked to have stayed longer or seen more but we touched the things that meant the most to me at that point in my life.

One of the most bewildering experiences came from sitting at our breakfast table in a little Bed and Breakfast home and observing two tourist couples at a nearby table. We were trying to figure out how we could get through another Irish breakfast that typically includes juice, eggs, bacon, sausage, scones, fresh jam, blood pudding, toast and either coffee or tea. One of the persons at the next table had brought a can of Coke to breakfast to help her start the day. They were decrying the fact that they had driven all the way from Sligo, the birthplace of the poet Yeats, to Donegal and back and had not seen even one place where they could find a hamburger. They were also upset and concerned that they had now gone three entire days without seeing the Dan Rather Evening News. When I commented to Wanda that they should be in Cleveland instead of Ireland, she suggested that we finish our tea in the sitting room by the fireplace. It was a good suggestion.

We knew we wanted to travel the country and see some of the things we had only heard about but I wanted to spend my actual birthday in a very ordinary but very real Irish locale. Some friends had recommended the little town of Portumna and suggested that would fit the bill perfectly. They had relatives that ran a Bed and Breakfast place and helped us make the arrangements. Mary ran the place.

She had four children ranging in age from twelve to two. She ran an impeccably clean place with six guest rooms, cooked the breakfasts for all the guests as well as for her family, managed the four children and kept her husband in line. She also worked part time at the local pub during the slow season. With all of that on her plate, she still found time to arrange a special Happy Birthday gig for the visitors from Canada.

When Wanda and I had returned from supper, Mary presented us with a birthday cake and an Irish dancing show put on by her two oldest, Marian and Lisa. Gary, who was about five, at the time, didn't want much to do with the dancing but was busy exploding around the room trying to work off the energy that is stored in most five year olds. The energy level was also fuelled by getting the largest piece of birthday cake and by chasing his little brother David. It was a busy room.

Mary warned Gary to settle down a number of times.

"Gary, settle down." No reaction.

"Gary, stop running and sit down." No reaction.

"Gary, come here and sit by me and stop playing the fool." No reaction.

Finally, the big threat was delivered. "Gary, do you remember the swat you got this morning?"

The reaction was instantaneous. Total stop from Gary, a fast look for a place to sit down immediately, very big eyes looking at Mom and the words spoken with the solemnity of a Shakespearean actor, "Oi do indeed, Mom".

They were birthday party words to live by and remember. Mary, showing just the slightest concern then said to us, "Now, you wouldn't be talking to the Social Services people about this little exchange would you?"

Mary, your secret rests with us.

There May be Ghosts

They, whoever "they" are, claim there are more ghosts in and around Gettysburg, Pennsylvania than any other place in the world. The three day battle, that was the turning point in the American Civil War, left more dead on the battlefield than any other U.S. engagement in history. The ghosts of the soldiers are said to still walk the battlefield.

Gettysburg is one of my favourite places. Wanda and I first visited the town and battlefield when we were on a trip to Williamsburg. Williamsburg was the first capitol in the American colonies. They still fly the British Union Jack over the restored Governor's Palace. The Americans don't quite get that part of the attraction.

Anyway, we were on our way to Williamsburg when we spotted some of the statues and cannons that are scattered about the Gettysburg battlefield area. It looked like an interesting place. We found accommodation. We ate at a great Pennsylvania Dutch restaurant. We checked out the electric map and battlefield museum. We saw where Lincoln put the finishing touches on his famous speech and generally had a good time. Gettysburg is primarily history with large amounts of tacky souvenir shops thrown in for good measure. But it's history told well.

We enjoyed it so much that when Paul and Laura were married and let us know they were taking a motor trip into that area we arranged a night's lodging in a battlefield motel so that they could also get a look at the town. They came back fans as well.

Every time Wanda and I had occasion to travel in or through that area, I insisted that we stop in Gettysburg. We've visited it in the Summer, in the Spring and in the Fall. I always wanted to take enough time on each trip to re-visit some museum or some part of the battlefield. I always saw something I had never seen before or learned a little more about Civil War history. I thought it was great.

I didn't realize how boring it had become for Wanda until I noted that she made sure any of our trips into the U.S. took us west from Buffalo and nowhere near Gettysburg.

"I've had a snoot full of cannons and statues of horses," she declared. "I don't ever want to see the electric map again. I don't ever again want to see Lincoln in a wax museum rising out of the floor while someone plays a tape of the Battle Hymn of the Republic."

I was shocked. How could you claim that you had seen enough of a little town of fewer than five thousand permanent residents after you've only visited it twelve times, I wondered. What's the matter with the woman?

At one time the highway from Harrisburg to Washington ran through Gettysburg. There is now a high speed by-pass road around the town. I think Wanda had something to do with its planning and construction. The last time we drove past the town, I insisted that I had to go into Gettysburg to make a washroom stop. She made me turn right around and drive directly back to the by-pass. She refused to even consider my argument that it may be shorter to just drive through the town rather than going back out to the high speed road. She's on to me.

When I learned that nephew Jim, another Civil War buff, had never been to Gettysburg, all the bells went off. If I can organize Jim, I thought, I can go there again. The trip was on.

It was a long weekend weekend with just the two of us. Based on my extensive experience with the area, I was the designated tour guide. Of course I had to show him the electric map and battlefield museum. Of course we stood where Lincoln delivered his famous Gettysburg address. Of course we followed the battlefield trail and stopped and read almost every plaque and admired the statues of horses and bad generals. We wandered the cemeteries and pondered the stupidity of war.

We sat in the old town square and conjured up pictures of soldiers and wagons and cannons and frightened townspeople. We went to Mass in an old Church that was used as a hospital for both sides during the battle. They opened the service by singing the old hymn of the time, "Amazing Grace". It was awesome, but only if you're into that sort of stuff. We were.

I gather, from listening to Jim's wife Renate, that Jim would bend the ear of anyone who would listen to him about what he saw and did at Gettysburg. If the town bites you, you become a bore about it. Some time after we got back, Jim told Renate that his doctor, who was doing some monitoring, told Jim that instead of seeing him every second week he would only be seeing him once every four months. Renate asked Jim if that was because the doctor was tired of hearing his stories about Gettysburg?

Jim said, "Actually, the doctor said he never wanted to see me again. I had to talk him into the four months."

Late in the afternoon of the second day of our visit, we came across a quiet glen that I had never noticed before. We got out of the car to read the story that was set out on the plaque. We learned that this place was where the final attack of the three day battle had taken place. The entire Federal contingent that was ordered to attack, had been wiped out in the space of less than ten minutes. As we read the plaque, we both noticed there was absolute silence. There was no wind, no rustling trees, no birds singing or insects buzzing. It was an absolute cold, eerie ghostly silence. We decided we should move along. As we moved away from the area the normal sounds you always hear in the countryside started again.

When I told Wanda about our rather ghostly experience she informed me, in no uncertain terms, "There may be ghosts at Gettysburg but it will never be mine. I've seen enough of the place."

Bottom of the Hole

I went to work for a construction company on a temporary basis while I waited for another job to open. Fourteen years later I bought the company. Twelve years after that the bank put the company into bankruptcy and told me to start over. I did.

One of the most difficult things about going through a business failure was thinking about all the great things that were done and all the great people I met over the years when the business was rocking along. Being in business for yourself is always tough. You do a lot of things and wear a lot of hats. You learn to not make excuses and you learn that you are required to do a lot of things yourself as you don't have the luxury of keeping other people available just in case you need them.

I don't have much use for banks. It's hard to respect an organization that would shut you down the week before Christmas because your collection of accounts is too slow. I have more respect for unions even though some of my most memorable fights took place over union positions. I was never very nice to the union representatives because I found they left you alone and moved along to bother the people that would sit and buy them a cup of coffee if you weren't too friendly. It was an effective time saving strategy. Most times union representatives, in the construction world, recognized when they were defending a jerk or a stupid position. They would give the defence the proper amount of lip service then move on before it became a war and before both sides were taking casualties. Public service unions have trouble grasping that concept.

We had a union employee working for the construction company as a carpenter. He was the kind of person you can find in almost any organization who is constantly looking for ways to take the absolute maximum while giving the absolute minimum. This particular person had raised that attitude to an art form and was moving on to trying to convince his fellow workers to pick up the same attitude. I decided the most effective way of dealing with him was to isolate him from the other workers.

I went out and purchased a large block of the hardest wood I could find and a supply of ardox style nails. I put the block of wood on the sunny side of our office trailer and told the individual to spend the morning driving the nails into the hardwood. In the afternoon, after the sun had swung around to the other side of the trailer, I had him move the block back into the sun side and pull the nails out. The next day we repeated the process. It was tough, hard, hot work but it was carpenter work that fell clearly under the contract.

After two days of such nonsense the union representative showed up to deal with a filed complaint. I bought him a coffee. He agreed that the driving and removal of nails was part of a carpenter job description and he agreed it was within the contract. He also convinced his union member that as he was consigned to that job it might be better if, together, they found him some other place to work. Ironically, the carpenter, the union representative and me all wound up being reasonably good friends over the years.

We were in the pile driving business. That meant that you could be working at ground level, at water level, a hundred feet in the air or seventy-five feet underground. I like to have my feet on the ground but you don't always get to do what you like to do.

Sometimes you get to do things you don't like to do simply to make a point. I remember going out to a jobsite with a veteran superintendent, on a Saturday, to measure something that was attached to the end of a crane boom. I didn't realize, until we got to the jobsite, that the crane boom was still a hundred feet in the air and that I was expected to climb up the attached pile leads to take the measurements the superintendent needed. It was a slow, terrifying climb up and a slow, terrifying climb down. It was not where a person who likes his feet on the ground wanted to be. I don't know what point I was making but I guess I established something about myself.

We were involved in doing a job at a steel mill that involved augering caissons approximately seventy-five feet deep. The jobsite was immediately beside the Hamilton Bay that had a water depth of approximately thirty feet. This meant that the bottom of the caisson was forty-five feet below the water that was immediately adjacent to the jobsite.

The construction process of the caissons involved driving a thirty-six inch diameter steel pipe approximately forty feet into the ground in order to seal the water off and to prevent it from flooding the caisson. The material inside the pipe would then be augered out and the hole would continue to be dug down to a depth of seventy-five feet. The bottom of the caisson would then be "belled out" to provide a larger base. The entire thing would then be cleared of all material and filled with concrete. Just before the concrete was poured, we would hang a protective liner of about thirty inches in diameter in the lower part of the shaft so that an inspector and a caisson worker could go down into the hole in a cage at the end of a crane line and clear out any small amounts of material that might still be left in place. Then the protective liners would be extracted before the concrete set.

The timing was always very critical because water would begin to seep into the hole if it was left open for any extended period of time. This would cause material to fall in from the unprotected sides and the caisson could collapse.

We were attempting to complete a caisson on a Friday afternoon and had run into an inspector that was convinced we were trying to build a watch instead of making a hole in the ground and filling it with concrete. He had taken a worker down into the hole three times and was never satisfied that all the loose dirt had been removed. He would not allow the concrete to be poured. I was made aware of the problem late Friday when the concrete company called and said they couldn't hold their trucks up much longer and that the caisson would either need to be poured quickly or wait until Monday. I knew if we tried to wait until Monday the caisson would collapse over the week-end and we would all be in a horrible mess.

I went to the jobsite and was told, very officiously, by the inspector that he and he alone was in charge. I hate being dealt with that way.

I suggested to the inspector that he and I should go down into the caisson to do an inspection. It was one of those times that I should have been listening instead of talking but he agreed to go. The construction crew started a pool to see how long it would be before I got agreement to let the concrete pour proceed and let the inspector out of the hole.

I was really ticked. The construction crew thought the entire thing was pretty funny. I told someone to order the concrete trucks because either the inspector would agree to the pour or only one of us would be coming out of the hole.

Then I got thinking, "these guys are all union people and, from time to time, we've had our differences. I'm about to go seventy-five feet into the ground in a tiny hole and I'm about to get there by standing in a wire cage attached to a single crane line. Then I expect the crane operator to pull me back out when I tug on the safety line." I was committed to the task but, I thought, I probably should be committed.

Then I thought of an incentive program. I went to the crane operator, the job foreman and all the crew and demanded that they give me their watches and their wallets. Friday was payday so I knew their wallets had value. When they asked me why I wanted them, I explained that I was taking them down into the hole with me as an incentive for them to make sure they pulled me back up. When you're seventy-five feet in the ground and you know you are also forty-five feet below the water table you want someone to have an incentive to get you back out. When you look up from the bottom it seems like you're looking up through a drinking straw. It's no place for a person who likes to have his feet on the ground.

The incentive program worked. The inspector and I got to the bottom of the hole where we had, what is described in diplomatic circles as, a frank and open exchange of views. After I had discussed his heritage and his intelligence and his chances of longevity, he approved the pour. The persons who had ten minutes in the pool were the winners but it felt like ten hours. The boys got their wallets and watches back. The inspector is probably out there making someone else crazy as we speak.

No, thank you very much. I don't need to have that experience again.

Island Fever

Television has been described as being "a vast wasteland". It's easy to see why, but occasionally you see something on television that touches a special chord. I was channel surfing around and came across a piece that took me back to an episode in my life that left me burning with shame and embarrassment. It was a documentary about monkeys and how they deal with problem solving.

I've described some of Hawaii and some of the things we saw and did during our first visit to Hawaii in my story about Captain Bean's Boat. We enjoyed the islands so much that Wanda and I arranged a vacation with her sister and husband so that we could see more. We arranged for hotel rooms on Oahu for the first week so that we would be right in the middle of everything and then arranged a very quiet condo on the island of Kauai for the second week. It turned out to be just about the best vacation we had ever taken.

When the trade winds are blowing, you awaken every day secure in the knowledge that the winds, which are more like breezes, will help keep the temperature at about seventy-four degrees and that it will be nice and sunny until late in the afternoon. The temperature will then fall all the way down to about seventy-two degrees and the breezes will also drop slightly. There is no word in the Hawaiian language for "weather" as they don't know about much different weather than what I have just described. It lulls you into pleasantly accepting what is known as "island fever".

Island fever causes your brain to slow significantly. The slower working of the brain then causes your reflexes to slow, your good judgement to fade, your ambition to disappear and after all that has kicked in, lethargy takes over. In an attempt to fight off the effects of island fever Paul and I tracked down a great happy hour in a little bar not far from our hotel. Wanda and Laura liked the idea of having a little down time every afternoon and then, after catching a nap, they would sort themselves out and get ready for dinner and a night out. Paul and I took that time as an opportunity to enjoy our own form of down time. We were required to walk through the International Marketplace to reach our happy hour bar and we would arrange and pay for fresh flowers for the ladies. We knew we would be late and rushed for time when we came back through the Marketplace, but the flower vendor would have our purchases ready for us and would hand them to us with a big "Aloha" and a smile as we were flying back to pick up the ladies for dinner.

Some people believe that Happy Hour means that the drinks are half price. When on vacation, I have come to believe that Happy Hour means you get two drinks for the price of one. There is a fundamental difference between those two philosophies. Paul and I had made the decision to try to fight the effects of island fever with Vodka and Pineapple juice, in my case, and with Rye and Ginger in his. I taught him the trick of ordering the first drink and seriously over-tipping the bartender. DeeDee, who more or less became our personal bartender, then looked after us in the grandest style by protecting our barstools and by over pouring every drink we ordered for the rest of the week. We found this to be a great idea. In retrospect, I can see that it fit clearly under the island fever symptom of "fading good judgement". However, it seemed like a good idea at the time.

We encountered another symptom of island fever when Paul and I tried to cross the main street behind Waikiki Beach. It is a very busy street and we found a pedestrian crosswalk with a button that was to be pushed to cause the light to change in your favour. We pushed the button and watched as the light turned from "Don't Walk" to "Walk". It took enough time to get the changed instruction to register in our stricken brains and to then get the instruction to proceed to get from our brains to our feet, that we missed the light. We tried a second time and missed again so we decided there was enough to see on our side of the street and gave up the crossing as a bad idea. Island fever had taken hold.

One evening, after our usual Happy Hour trip followed by a nice dinner with a little wine and an after dinner liqueur, we made our way back to our hotel. The ladies decided they had had enough of the fast life and went upstairs to their rooms. Paul and I had spied a line-up of Hawaiian shirted men and muumuued ladies waiting outside the nightclub area of our hotel. We inquired what they were waiting for and were told that they were part of a Senior's Tour and that the nightclub entertainment was one of their stops. As we were properly attired in our Hawaiian shirts I convinced Paul that we should just tag onto the tour group, see if we can get into the nightclub that way and see what happens. It was an easy sell to Paul, which proved again that good judgment was fading, if not already totally gone.

We got into line. We looked straight ahead when we were being marched into the nightclub. We were ushered to a ringside table and we were almost immediately approached by a beautiful waitress with a flower in her hair, a short skirt and an Hawaiian lei around her neck.

"Are you two fellas part of the tour?" she asked.

"We certainly are", I replied.

"Then you're entitled to two ordinary drinks or one exotic drink as part of the tour package", she explained.

"Is Vodka and Pineapple juice an ordinary drink or an exotic drink?" I asked.

"That's considered an exotic drink," she said.

"I don't see why it should be", I said. "It's just a mixed drink that gets served all over the islands. It doesn't have an umbrella in it," I argued.

"I'll go check", she said and she was off.

"What on God's earth are you doing?", asked Paul. His tan seemed to have faded somewhat as he sat in on the bi-play between myself and the waitress.

"Vodka and Pineapple juice shouldn't be considered an exotic drink", I replied. "They're trying to rip me off because the tour people are allowed two ordinary drinks."

"We're not on the tour, you jerk", he sputtered. "You're going to get us arrested".

Right at that time, our waitress returned and admitted that Vodka and Pineapple juice was indeed an ordinary drink and that as a tour member I was allowed two. Paul said he would have the same.

"You don't drink Vodka", I said to Paul.

"I can't think. I just want to get out of here before the cops arrive", he answered.

The drinks were refreshing. The waitress was pleasant. The people on the tour were friendly. It was a good floor show. It was a nice night. Paul figured we better get out of town so we moved on to Kauai the next day.

The Marriott, Hilton and Sheraton people have long since found Kauai. When we visited that island it was pre-development and pre-tourist. When we checked into our condo that had been paid for in advance they wondered why I thought we should fill out a registration card. Who bothers? When I asked for a key to our place the two people in the combination laundry room and lobby looked at each other and shrugged. Who bothers?

The island had one traffic light but not too many people paid attention to it. The island had two power failures per day but no one seemed to notice. The condo doors were made of Japanese rice paper but who cares? It was laid back. There were no Hawaiian shirt factories and no night club tours. If you wanted to have wine with your dinner you brought it with you.

One evening we had dinner in a converted plantation house. There was a large veranda that surrounded the house. The big old ceiling fans provided some Hemingwayesque atmosphere. The Pacific lapped against the nearby beach. The temperature stayed at its usual seventy-two degrees. The seafood was great. The waiter was a beach bum who carried food occasionally in order to keep himself in surfboard wax. We had more than a couple of "pops" but that didn't present a problem as Wanda accepted the designated driver role.

The bill was hand written and hand calculated. We noticed that the waiter, who was pleasant but low voltage, was having trouble getting the bill added up. He explained that he had added the bill four times and that he had got four different answers.

I said, "give me the bill and I'll add it for you." I did that and compared my total with his and discovered that we now had five different answers.

Paul volunteered, "Give it to me and I'll add it."

We then, of course, had six different answers and it was getting late.

I suggested to the waiter, "Let me add up the six different answers. We'll average them and then pay the average."

"I think I can sell that to the boss", and did.

It was a laid back island.

A couple of evenings later we made the mistake of buying a large bottle of a very cheap "Hearty Burgundy" wine and took it with us for dinner at Bruce's Spaghetti House. It was probably a memorable evening but the following morning Paul and I were moving slowly and with care. We decided that it had better be an easy day around the condo.

There was a coconut producing palm tree outside the door of our residence. A number of coconuts had fallen and had been collected in a bin beside the tree. We decided that we would open a coconut and treat ourselves to the result of living off the land.

Paul and I husked and cut and pulled and hammered at a coconut for four hours. We re-positioned twice in order to stay in the shade as the sun moved through the day. We used every kitchen utensil we could find that had a point or cutting edge. We broke half of them. Finally, after skinning several knuckles, developing huge blisters and cutting several fingers each, we had husked the coconut. It looked to be about the size of a tennis ball by the time the outside protection had been removed. It only took us six hours but we had food and fresh coconut juice. In fact, we had approximately one half a small fruit juice glass of coconut milk and we only had to share it among four people. It was a very productive day.

The entire episode, pain and all, flashed before my eyes as I watched the television documentary about monkeys. The monkeys were opening coconuts to feed themselves. They would take a ripe coconut, climb a tree and drop the coconut on a hard piece of ground. If it didn't crack the husk, they would repeat the process. Before long the nut part would appear. They would then bang it against another hard object and, lo and behold, within minutes they were drinking coconut milk and eating coconut meat.

It was embarrassing but, I guess you can learn a lot from television and from monkeys.

Holy Jingles

I was only fired once in my life. I was thirteen at the time and I was fired by Mr. H., the owner of a small neighbourhood drugstore.

Mr. H. was a really good guy. He had served with the Canadian army in WWII. He walked quickly and always stood straight as a ramrod. He never cussed and when faced with a cussing situation he fell back upon his phrase "Holy Jingles". This was as bad as it got.

He was a tough boss. I once lost a ten dollar bill when I was on a delivery for the store. A ten dollar loss was a major deal when you were earning ten dollars per week for working every day after school from four o'clock until nine and working either Saturday or Sunday from noon until six. It was a big loss for the store as well when they were selling Pepsi for seven cents and a package of cigarettes for thirty-three cents.

I didn't get fired for losing the money but there was no way I was off the hook. Mr. H., who I always referred to as "Mister", deducted two dollars per week from my pay until the loss was restored. Gradually, I was promoted from delivery boy to stock boy to soda jerk to counter service. I was on the road to success and I got a discount on the ice cream I bought. Mr. H. always made sure it was bought and not just eaten. I told you he was tough.

Although I had received all those promotions and, occasionally, was even left to tend the store myself I still held all the jobs and filled in at whatever needed to be done. I was quick at math and I thought that was a good thing. In those days well before automated cash registers that tote up everything that's shown on a bar code, produces a receipt and pays out the change, we accomplished those same tasks by writing down each price on the carrying bag and adding up the numbers. We then actually needed to count out the change and smile at the customer. How quaint!

I had just arrived back in the store from some deliveries and found Mr. H. totally overwhelmed with customers. For some reason they were lined up three deep at the check out area. Springing into action I started to take the purchases from various customers and, because we were so busy, I just added the purchases mentally, gave them the total, took the money and moved on. Mr. H. continued to write the purchase amounts on the paper bags he was using as per usual. I would wait until he had written down the amount and would give him the total having added them mentally as he was writing them down. What a team, I thought.

When the rush was over and we were balancing the cash for the day he turned to me and said, "you're fired."

"What do you mean I'm fired", I protested. "What did I do?"

"You showed me up" was his answer. "I don't need a smart show-off. You're finished."

I had no idea what he was talking about or what I had done wrong. All I knew is that I no longer had a job I both liked and needed. I had heard about this 'life isn't fair' thing but it hit with a thud.

A few days later I received a message from him saying that he wanted me back, 'provided I had learned my lesson.' I didn't know what I had done wrong so I also didn't know what lesson I was supposed to have learned but I agreed that I had learned it in order to get back to work. I'm really glad the lesson was learned otherwise I would not have been witness to what was probably Mr. H's most embarrassing moment.

This all took place in the dark ages before colour TV if you can imagine such a time. Someone had invented the aerosol spray can.

I was in the store alone when a salesman left a sample of an aerosol shaving cream. He explained how it was dispensed and demonstrated the nice handful of shaving foam that appeared like magic from the tin ready to go. I just left the tin sitting on the counter and had forgotten about it when Mr. H. returned from his dinner.

A customer came and, saw the tin and asked Mr. H. what it was.

"It looks like one of those new fangled shaving creams", said Mr. H.

"How does it work?"

"I'm not sure", said Mr. H. "Let's give it a try."

He removed the cap. He aimed the tin and pushed the valve. Unfortunately, the nozzle was aimed directly at our rather well dressed customer and the valve was pushed to full speed. A great arc of white foam flew across the counter. It started at the bottom of our customer's nice jacket, advanced up his tie and ended at his collar.

"Holy Jingles", said Mr. H. grabbing a towel. I don't recall what happened next because I just disappeared into the storeroom and stuffed a towel into my mouth. I had already been fired once and that was enough. I do recall that even though it was the coming thing, Mr. H. never stocked aerosol products and refused to discuss why.

Several years later I stopped by for a visit and to see how he was getting along. I still called him Mr. H. We had a great visit and he seemed to enjoy the fact that one of his old delivery boys would think enough of him to stop in for a visit. I had a Pepsi.

When I was leaving, after exchanging a lot of good memories and a few laughs Mr. H. said, "that will be ten cents." I told you he was tough.

Partnership

It's a rainy Mothers Day. Wanda has heard from her three children and is pleased. She couldn't play golf today and is displeased. We've been married for forty-five years at our 2002 anniversary.

Wanda and I met each other when I was eighteen years old. I fell in love with her and asked her, three weeks later, if she would marry me. She thought I was totally nuts and told me so. I put her down as "undecided".

In one way or another I've been selling things all my life. I made the greatest sale of my career when, three years after first being asked, she showed up at the Church and we left as man and wife. We had a reception in the back room of the Charles Coffee Shop. I missed part of it because the Boston Red Sox, with my hero Ted Williams, were televised in the next door bar and I slipped out to watch part of the game. My friend Ted came and got me. He told me I was nuts for doing such a thing. I explained that I had already been told that by Wanda.

Three children, two rented apartments, six houses including two rentals, one bankruptcy and two careers for me along with one career for Wanda and we are still celebrating anniversaries.

I've put down some stories and expressed some feelings at the urging of some friends. As I've re-read the stories, one of the things that comes through to me is that Wanda has helped me live a very fun and sometimes remarkable life. She has been the person that has caused me to grow and somehow managed to trick me into thinking that I was responsible for whatever has become of me.

Very often when we are just sitting and talking, I've remarked that I never seem to be able to impress her. Of course I can't impress her. When I re-read so many of my own stories it's easy to conclude that it would be hard for me to impress anyone. Then she makes me re-think again and I conclude that together we have done some really good things. It's a partnership and I've probably got a lot better partner than she does.

If you take the time to read some of the stories you may find that there is an understanding of deep love and affection for the person that has let me bounce through life. I hope I managed to convey that message.

When I come home from the hunt of life thumping my chest and bragging about this, that or the other thing, she lets me. When the balloon gets too full of hot air she lets some out. I don't always like that but it needs to be done. When I come home having been thumped with nothing to brag about, she somehow manages to get me some room and to get some air back into the balloon. We call it "living to fight another day" but you need a partner to make it work.

Wanda, I will never get the choice of what shirt goes with what pants quite right. I will always wind up with an occasional sweater on backwards. I will always tend to march towards the sound of gunfire and get myself into trouble. I will always be just a little out of step with the rest of the world. I will never really enjoy dancing.

I wish I could write a love story because I've been able to live one. Sometimes the right words just can't be found.

Midnight at Christmas

Does a tree that falls in an empty forest make a noise? Logically, the answer must be yes but no one has had the first hand experience of knowing whether or not the premise is correct.

John Denver did a song that talked about the possibility of animals being able to talk. The song has a line that says, "how can you be sure that animals can't talk just because they have never spoken to you."

Christmas has always been a special time for me. The special feeling doesn't come from the religious side, although that is there too, but it comes from the extra effort that people put out to be nice. I wish we could bottle that feeling and haul some of it out at various times throughout the year.

For a number of years I took Adam and Kate to the Children's Mass on early Christmas Eve. I really enjoyed it and enjoyed the good feeling that came from being with them at a special time. The highlight of the Children's Mass is the pageant that re-enacts the birth of Christ. The enjoyment, for me, comes from seeing the pride of the parents, the panic of the teachers in charge of putting the pageant together and the halo of some angel, somewhere among the group, that is slightly askew or has fallen off entirely.

When Kate and Adam were really small they also had the big eyes as they took in the show. They also, hopefully, got the same good feeling as I did when they took gifts and put them under the tree for less fortunate kids. Hopefully, they felt good about grampa and hopefully, understood how warm grampa felt about them.

One year I had taken Kate and Linda to see the rock musical Jesus Christ Superstar. We all thought it was great, including grampa, who was trying to figure out how a rock musical ties in with the Big Guy. It does. A few days later Kate went to the Christmas Children's Mass with me. Again, I was quite taken by the entire effort.

As we were leaving I said to the local junior priest, "That was quite a show father. I took the kids to see Jesus Christ Superstar last week and this was every bit as good."

He was quite taken aback at my brash comparison and responded, "This is not a show."

I suggested to him, "Father, you just don't quite get it about life do you?" It was a strange little exchange and I guess it shows again that I go to Church because I'm bad and not because I'm good.

We have good friends that invite us over to visit with them and their friends on Christmas Eve and we value the invitations. For years, while we lived on the farm, we invited friends to stop by on Christmas Eve and we had some great visits. I always tried to position myself close enough to the radio so that I could hear "Paul Reid's Christmas" for the umpteedumth time. I still get caught up in the story about the littlest angel and the story of the watch fob and the combs. It was just part of Christmas. The gatherings would usually break up around ten o'clock as people had other places to go or things to do at home.

There is an old legend that tells believers that on Christmas Eve at midnight, animals can talk with each other, provided there is no one around to hear them.

Once people left our little soiree, I always took Tammara, Dan and Linda, gathered a pocket full of carrots, bundled up and went up to say goodnight to the animals. It was the only night of the year we would make that kind of visit.

The animals were usually quite settled by that time and we knew we would be disturbing them just a little bit. We would take the dogs with us and go over and break all the rules by throwing down some extra feed for the cows then petting and talking with the horses while we gave them their carrot treats. The dogs were always just pleased to be out for an extra walk.

Then we would leave them with stall doors open so that they would be left alone just in case they could talk to one another at midnight. I don't know that they didn't just because I never heard them.

Then the kids would go to bed so that they could be up at four to check their gifts then go back to bed secure in the knowledge that Mom and Dad would never know they had been up. Mom and Dad would finish their chores and toast another year.

I wanted to celebrate my sixty-fifth birthday in Ireland and I did. Before we left on the trip, Linda gave me an envelope marked, "not to be opened until June 16, 2001". It was a great Happy Birthday and said, in part,

"I would like to thank you for being the Easter Bunny who ate my carrots and the Santa who wrote me the "yes Linda, there is a Santa Claus" letter. For taking me out on Christmas Eve to say goodnight to the animals with a treat and leaving their doors open so they could talk. You taught me faith and hope, though I didn't realize it at the time."

Those were good visits on Christmas Eve.

Hotel Suisse

We decided to take up skiing. I was born in Timmins and my mother took pride in telling everyone that she would put me out in a carriage, in below zero temperatures, to have my afternoon nap. I don't know what that was supposed to do for me. I think it just caused me to hate the cold.

Nevertheless, if you're sentenced to living in Canada from December through March you better do something to counter cabin fever. We took up skiing.

We started on little area hills. It was fun if you call landing on your fanny fun. We would drive to the ski hills in the Orangeville area most weekends and, with our friends, we would beat our way up and down the hills for several hours. Fortunately, apart from a few scrapes and bruises, we never got hurt. It kept us in better shape, it made us very hungry and we had a great time. It speeded up winter.

Three couples decided we would put together a ski holiday in the Quebec Laurentians. We were barely beyond the novice stage of skiing but it sounded like a good idea at the time. Some of us were barely able to negotiate our way up a rope tow but we knew we could handle whatever was thrown at us. Falling up a hill is really a disgrace.

We selected a small resort called Hotel Suisse. We felt it was large enough to support a reasonable ski lesson program but small enough to avoid the resort factory-like atmosphere. We made a stop in Montreal, where we were introduced to corned beef sandwiches at Ben's Delicatessen, then we were on our way to a three bedroom chalet at Hotel Suisse.

The following morning after a huge breakfast, we gathered at the foot of the main ski hill and were sorted out into various classes that reflected our skill levels. Each person in our party of six wound up in a different class. This was probably a good thing because we could each hide our failures from the others and bring back tales of derring-do without fear of contradiction.

As the week wore on we all acquired some noticeable skiing skills. Given what they had to work with, the instructors were obviously outstanding. The hills we passed on the drive in, no longer seemed as steep or as high. The instructions, when followed, seemed to work most of the time. We could stop when we wanted. We could traverse. We could ride the fall line for a while. We could ski moguls. We could enjoy.

My class instructor was named Herman Schmidt. Herman claimed to have once been a member of the Austrian National Ski Team. That might have been true because he was quite an accomplished skier. He was also blessed with a Germanic/Teutonic sense of humour that could best be described as "no sense of humour at all". I know that my sense of humour caused Herman great pain as he struggled to figure out what I thought was funny. He never succeeded.

The food was great at Hotel Suisse. We would be up at the crack of dawn for breakfast. We would ski from eight o'clock until noon. We would meet in the lounge for lunch and wolf down huge hero sandwiches while warming ourselves around a pot bellied stove. Wanda would march up to the dining room and demand a bowl of chowder and a plate of stew. It didn't matter how much we ate because we would ski it off between one o'clock and five o'clock when it started to get dusk.

We would then make our way back to the chalet, eat a few hors d'oeuvres, tell a few lies, have a couple of pops then go to the dining room and eat an enormous gourmet dinner. We managed all of this and no one ever put on an ounce. Those were the days my friend, as they say in the song.

We skipped most of the organized evening entertainment as we were either too tired or too full, or both. One evening, however, they showed a film on downhill ski racing. The cameras were attached to the helmets of the skiers and it was really very spectacular. The following morning our instructor Herman decided to teach us how to handle high speed check turns. For some reason that I can't fathom now, I agreed to take the lesson. Like I really need to know anything about high speed check turns.

Herman stood at the very top of a severe drop covered with moguls. He explained the procedure. We then watched as he demonstrated the moves and slammed to a stop half way down the hill. We were to do the manoeuvres then stop in front of Herman so that he could critique our moves.

I was about the third or fourth to go. I was terrified but peer pressure moves you along. Before I could talk myself out of it I was launched and hurtling. The snow was a blur. The check part of the check turn procedures didn't seem to have much effect. The turn part didn't seem to have much effect either but I was still on my feet and I was a survivor. I blew to a stop in front of Herman with snow flying in all directions and waited for my praise.

He brushed off some snow and looked at me with generations of Germanic disapproval in his glare and said, "Pat, did you go to the movie about downhill racers?"

"Sure did Herman. It was great."

"Today, Pat, I am teaching check turns."

"I know, Herman", I responded, "and I think I've got it."

I wish I could properly describe the furrowed brow and the worried look that can overtake an Austrian ski instructor as he sees his entire professional teaching career melting away. I saw that look and, just for a second, I agonized for Herman. I had his full attention. It was as if there were only the two of us on the hill. He drew himself up to his full 5'7" and in a sad voice said,

"Pat, you came straight down that hill like a downhill racer. There were no checks and no turns, except maybe in your head."

I didn't know what to say so, for once, I said nothing. Herman continued in the same serious tone.

"Soon you will leave this place. You will go to some other place to ski. You will ski there like you ski here this morning. Then, someday, someplace, you will fly off a trail and be killed. When they find you in the Spring, people will gather around and they will say "That man was taught to ski at Hotel Suisse by Herman Schmidt." '

Herman saw it as a sad end to a great teaching career. I hate being held responsible for such a career breaker. I admit, Herman had a good case.

Encore

Turning Sixty-Five

There are several landmark birthdays. Becoming a teen-ager is a target so turning thirteen is extra important. For some reason, turning sixteen is a big one. Usually that's associated with the rite of passage that comes from being able to legally drive a car. Eighteen gets you legally carded in many jurisdictions so you can now officially order a beer. In some places, that next step in the rite of passage is delayed to age twenty-one.

Age thirty is less important for most people but seems more important to ladies than men. One of the depressing realizations that comes with the thirtieth birthday is that it has been a long time since you were last asked to produce identification when you ordered a drink. Forty is traumatic for many people. They start to think about all they had read about middle age. They also start to check on the numbers of persons they know that are age eighty and re-define middle age.

Fifty-five starts to get you a number of special seniors discounts. This is a major crossroads. Some people can hardly wait to fess up to being fifty-five so that they can save twenty percent on senior days at the mall. Others refuse to feel fifty-five and, therefore, refuse the discounts as a matter of principle. I went broke at the age of forty-eight and started my economical life over at that age. By the time I reached fifty-five I was too busy to take notice. Wanda did an even better job of ignoring that particular landmark.

I remember how impressed I was as I watched my friend Archie start a brand new engineering business in his late forties. I thought, wow, a lot of people are starting to think about winding down and here's Archie starting something brand new when he's so old. I was twenty-five at the time so persons in their late forties seemed really old. Now they're all young pups at that age.

Sixty-five has been the landmark birthday. It wasn't a case of feeling old or getting morbid about actuarial tables. It was more a realization that you had best keep things sorted out a little more carefully and that you had best get things done that you felt were important. I had run out of excuses for not visiting Ireland and decided that is where I would be when

I turned sixty-five. It was a very good decision. Prior to leaving for Ireland, I was given a card by a good friend that read, "You are a good person". You need that when you're taking inventory at age sixty-five and it was more than just very much appreciated.

If you are fortunate enough to reach the sixty-five year landmark, you get the opportunity of taking a little more time with your family and friends. You get to hug the grandkids a little more often. You get to talk to your family a little differently, knowing that everyone has a little different perspective at that point. You may get to mend, or attempt to mend, a few fences. You appreciate friends and family more and you try to tell them. You take out and re-read the "You are a good person card". You get to do some things that you might have put off for too long.

I once heard a Priest, in a retirement area of the U.S., explain the large numbers of people that turned out for the Christmas Masses and the very heavy collection plates that ensued. He said it was very simple. "They're cramming for their finals."

Perhaps it's that, or perhaps it's as simple as Adlai Stevenson once said when asked what he wanted to do most after a tiring loss in his run for the U.S. Presidency. He said, "I just want to sit in the shade of a tree and watch people dance."

By the time you pass sixty-five you have probably spent much too much time boring people with your stories. You may find that you have been sent away with the suggestion that you write some of them down so that they might read them when they feel like it. That's probably a good idea. That's what I've tried to do.

I hope it has been a fun read.

Thanksgiving Dance

One of the most feared questions that I can hear is "would you like to dance"?

I don't hear it often because I do everything within my power to avoid being put into the position where it becomes a logical question. We receive our fair number of invitations to weddings and special occasions so the question does get asked. Once or twice each year I try to respond in the affirmative and Wanda and I have managed an annual dance for many years.

We came from a family of non-huggers. As I've gotten older I have found myself with several more huggers than I once had and it is, I admit, an enjoyable experience. I can't get the hang of "air kissing", nor do I see the sense of it, but hugging can be good. Dancing seems to be neither hugging nor air kissing so it comes across, to me, as a bad exercise. Churchill once described golf as "a good walk spoiled". I find dancing a good hug wasted.

At one point in my life I found myself the campaign manager for a local Federal candidate. As campaign manager you get to do most of the organizing and you get to avoid most of the public involvement. I was once asked if I would ever be interested in running for Parliament. I responded with a "yes" but only if it didn't involve running in an election. I'm sure there are a lot of good people that have arrived at the same conclusion.

Nevertheless, being a campaign manager can be fun. It's especially fun when your candidate is not expected to win as this lets you do all kinds of things on a "maybe this will work" basis while knowing that if it doesn't work, you weren't supposed to succeed anyways.

Our candidate was not expected to win. There were those that expected with me as campaign manager, there was definitely no chance that our guy could win. We just kept doing things that seemed right and, before we knew it, we were in the race. We had it figured out that the best strategy was to smile, wave and nod while pretending not to be able to hear any really difficult questions. The second part of the strategy was to keep moving along to the next engagement. Once you got stopped or settled you almost always started to get into trouble. Some so called politicians never seem to get this figured out.

One evening our last scheduled stop was at a Catholic convent. We were met by the head Nun and taken into her small office.

"You boys look tired" she said.

We allowed as how we were but this was our last scheduled meeting of the day.

"Perhaps then" she said, "you could use a little drink".

We allowed as how that sounded like a fine idea indeed and the good Sister set out to take care of the matter.

In her absence my guy observed that this type of hospitality could cause him to convert. At that point in my life I had been on a sabbatical of several years from the Catholic Church (my choice not theirs), but I agreed that we seemed to have hit an area of hospitality that I couldn't recall from my altar boy years.

She returned in a few minutes with two fruit juice glasses of apple juice. It was nice. It was appreciated. It made no converts. We presented her with a gift copy of the biography of Pope John XXIII which she graciously accepted, although she did tell us that it was the nicest copy of the book that she had received and that it would go into the convent library along with the previous twelve that had already been gifted to her. I made a mental note to try to be a little more original.

We had a nice meeting with some very nice people. Most of them voted for our candidate so the evening was well spent.

There were two lawyers that had been in partnership for years. They were great with each other and always got along famously, until an election was called. One of them was a staunch Liberal. The other was a staunch Conservative. Six weeks before any election day they stopped speaking to each other. The practice would grind to a complete halt as they both left lawyering behind and spent every waking moment campaigning for their respective candidates. They both lived in the same electoral riding so the competition was not only fierce, but personal.

They both attended the same Church, which happened to be the same Church I was not attending at that time. I don't know if you can technically not attend a Church but that is what I was not doing at that point in my life. Coincidentally, however, that particular Church held a Thanksgiving Day dance that was considered to be one of the social events of the year and was, therefore, a must do event for any political aspirant.

As campaign manager, I put the event on our calendar, arranged tickets and organized our wives so that we could mix and mingle and do the event. When we arrived at the very crowded Church Hall I discovered that our ally lawyer, for some reason, was not in attendance but that his very adversarial partner was very much in evidence and quite unhappy that we were unofficially campaigning at his Church's social.

It wasn't my place to be concerned about such an attitude. In fact, I had already approached a friendly member of the dance committee and suggested that our candidate could conduct the lucky number draw during intermission and bring greetings from Ottawa to the good citizens of Ancaster. The committeeman readily agreed.

At intermission our candidate took the stage, spent several minutes drawing prizes and hugging the lady prize winners. He made a fine short speech about about the record of his Government and brought the aforementioned greetings from the Prime Minister.

I was standing close to the very unhappy lawyer who was getter more and more agitated as the intermission unfolded with our candidate at centre stage. I overheard him grump to the person standing next to him:

"We don't see the guy from one end of the year to the next and he waltzes in here and completely takes over the place. This is outrageous" he fumed.

I moved over to him and said, "Come on, Len. Chill out a little. The guy is the sitting member of Parliament so it's perfectly logical that he be here and make a little speech. He spends most of his time in Ottawa, so naturally, you wouldn't expect to see him around here. Take it easy" I advised.

"I'm not talking about the guy on the stage" snapped Len. "I'm okay with him. It's you I'm talking about!"

Oops. Len probably had a very good point.

I found Wanda. I suggested that we perhaps, should have our annual dance and then I suggested we quietly move along. I hate being the bad guy when I don't even see it coming.

Don't Drink the Water

A lawyer friend once asked if we would like to take a vacation trip with he and his wife. I said sure. The next thing I knew, we were on a plane to Acapulco Mexico.

Once in Mexico, we learned a number of things very quickly.

We learned that the scene in the movie "Ten" where Dudley Moore is jumping from towel to towel because the beach sand is too hot to walk on, is absolutely accurate.

We learned that it made no difference if you are laying beside the pool or laying in the pool because the heat and water temperature are the same.

We learned that the practice of taking Siestas makes perfect sense because the heat will knock you flatter than a tortilla if you don't take a break.

We learned that almost everybody lies to you almost all of the time.

On our second day in Acapulco, we were introduced to Rudy. Rudy was a beautiful specimen of Mexican charm. He was graced with dark swarthy skin, greying hair, perfect white teeth, catlike grace as he moved and a twelve year old station wagon that he used to run tours. We met Rudy when we paid a significant sum of pesos to a person at a tour desk that promised us a delightful evening touring various Acapulco nightclubs. We paid extra because we wanted to avoid the typical tour bus or tour group. We were instructed to meet Rudy in our hotel lobby at 7:30 that evening for our exclusive and private nightclub tour.

Our lawyer friend was concerned about missing Rudy and suggested that we be in the lobby at 7:00 in case Rudy was early. I reminded our friend that no one had been early for anything yet in Mexico and that Rudy was not likely to be the exception to that rule. Nonetheless, to keep our friend happy, we met downstairs at 7:00.

We were dressed appropriately for the event. In other words, we were dressed like four sappy Mexican tourists. The men wore ruffled pastel coloured shirts and light coloured pants with white shoes. The ladies wore fancy wraparound skirts and wildly colourful blouses with flowers in their hair. We were a sight to behold.

Unfortunately, Rudy was not there at 7:00 o'clock to do the beholding. Nor was he there at 7:30. He wasn't there at 8:00 o'clock either and he wasn't there at 8:30. Our lawyer friend was getting especially concerned as he felt he had a substantial investment in Rudy, who we were yet to meet, and he was becoming more and more convinced that Rudy had taken the pesos and run.

Finally, close to nine o'clock, in strolled Rudy. He was gorgeous and was the perfect Mexican gentleman. Our lawyer friend immediately lit into the man with the words,

"Where have you been? We paid for a private tour starting at 7:30 and here it is, almost nine o'clock before you even show up!"

Rudy responded by flashing the big grin and said,

"Senor, please. Don't spoil my evening." We knew immediately where we stood in Rudy's scheme of things.

The four of us were then ushered into his twelve year old station wagon. Rudy then drove half a block down the street and stopped at another hotel.

"Why are we stopping here?" asked my lawyer friend.

"To pick up the other passengers", answered Rudy.

"This is supposed to be a private and exclusive tour" said our friend.

Again, we get the big Rudy grin.

"Before you came to Mexico" said Rudy, "what was the advice you were given about the country?"

"I guess it was, don't drink the water", answered our friend.

"That's right", said Rudy. "Do you know why tourists get that advice?"

"Because the water makes them sick?", ventured our friend.

"No", said Rudy. "Because the water makes you lie. That's what happens to those of us who live here."

We were then joined by four other tourists, who had also bought an exclusive nightclub tour. My friend and I sat at the very back of the wagon with our feet hanging out over the open tailgate. The other six people and Rudy, were jammed into the other two seats. We saw the cliff divers and Aztec acrobats. We did get marched in and out of three or four other nightclubs of various repute and wound up watching a performance of a tired and disinterested flamenco dancer. The evening left us a little too tired and carrying a little too much tequila but Rudy was an experience.

Sometime during the evening he explained a little about how the Acapulco bargaining system worked. In Acapulco, at the time, there were no fixed prices on anything. You bargained for the best taxi rate. You bargained over trinkets and market items. You bargained over food and clothes. Rudy explained that the vendor was generally expecting to receive approximately half of the opening asking price of the item under discussion.

If you were asked for 100 pesos, Rudy advised that you counter-offer at 25 pesos. The vendor would then probably drop his position to 75 pesos. You should then counter at close to 50 pesos. The deal would finally be struck at or about the 50 peso mark. In the meantime, as part of the process, you should expect much head shaking, hand waving, an occasional obscene gesture and some hand wringing.

We took his advice and over the remaining days of the holiday, found it worked quite effectively. Wanda found the process very annoying but the experience must have been good for her because she is among the best bargain hunters I've ever known.

The evening before we were to leave Acapulco, Wanda and I were walking back towards our hotel. We were in a bit of a hurry when we were approached by a street vendor offering hand crocheted white shawls.

Wanda remarked on their beauty and suggested we buy one to take home. Knowing that her comments had greatly weakened our bargaining position, and being in a bit of a hurry, I asked for the price.

"Two hundred pesos, senor" said the vendor.

Hoping to move the process along, I went immediately to the twenty-five percent offering position and responded, "fifty pesos."

"Sold", said the vendor.

"Dammit," said I.

"What's the matter?" Wanda asked.

"The fifty percent rule means that the vendor should have wanted one hundred pesos. The fact that he grabbed the fifty peso offer means that we've been had. We should have been able to buy them for less. Now we need to find another guy selling shawls."

"Why?" asked Wanda. "I wanted a shawl. I have a shawl."

"Because now I have to average down by buying more shawls at the right price," I explained.

"You are a weird person," I was told by my darling wife.

We found another shawl vendor. I managed to buy at a much lower price than fifty pesos and three persons in our family, much to their surprise, received Mexican shawls for Christmas.

The next morning, when we were making arrangements to go to the airport, one of our party was uncomfortably ill. We told the bus driver we would arrange a taxi rather than using the hotel bus transport. We were assured that the bus would leave the hotel in the next ten minutes and go directly to the airport. It would arrive, we were told, even sooner than a taxi. We believed him and boarded the bus. The bus then left our hotel, made a U turn and stopped at a hotel across the street. We waited a half hour while they boarded more passengers.

The bus driver that looked us straight in the eye and said we would go directly to the airport had obviously been drinking the water.

I Think It's Jim

I've observed over the years that women, much more than men, not only pay closer attention to instructions and detail but are much more likely to retain what they have heard and learned.

A man, when finally forced to ask for directions, will listen attentively but only retain the information up to and including the second item. If told, for example, that he should continue down the road to the second stoplight, then turn left until he comes to a gas station on his right, then turn left at the gas station until he comes to the white Church you can be almost guaranteed that the following will happen.

He will continue down the road to the second stoplight. He will turn left and then will see the gas station on his right. At that point, his mind will go blank. He could turn left. He could turn right. He could continue straight ahead. Whatever choice he makes, he will quickly lose confidence in it and return to the gas station to ask for further directions.

A woman, on the other hand, will willingly seek help with directions. She will listen carefully. She may even make notes or have the helper draw her a picture. She will then follow all those directions and, lo and behold, arrive at her destination on time with her blood pressure still close to normal.

The only time the system breaks down is when the woman gets the directions and then passes them on to her male companion. It is one of life's certainties that the passing along of directions from a woman to a man is always done with an air of superiority that makes men crazy. Under this scenario, they still arrive on time. Her blood pressure is still normal. His is not. They are seldom still speaking to each other.

A woman can walk into a party or a reception and without looking to either the left or the right could, if tested, tell you the colour of every dress. She could describe every hairstyle, every piece of jewellery and every matched up couple in the room. A man, on the other hand slips into a defensive trance and couldn't tell you, if his life was depending upon it, whether or not anyone was even wearing shoes.

Introductions are especially difficult. Wanda can be introduced to someone for the first time and within seven seconds of the introduction she can tell you the person's name, middle name, dog's name, children's names and the maiden name of the person's Aunt Sally. She also somehow knows that they had difficulty twenty-three years ago selling their second house in Calgary and that their nephew Jason just took a job in California with Microsoft.

On the other hand, if I'm introduced to someone I can look them straight in the eye. I can give them a firm but generous handshake. I can listen to their name very carefully and I can immediately call them by name in order to reinforce the learning experience. I can then walk three feet away and find that I must turn to Wanda and ask, "what's his name again?"

As I said earlier, I have no idea whether or not he's even wearing shoes.

I had gone a number of years without playing golf. We had retained our social membership at our club but with the pressures of helping raise a young family, running a business and managing a farm there was no time to play golf. I took the game up again at the urging of my son Dan and I renewed my playing membership. As I had gone quite a spell without golf connections, I found myself at the pro shop asking the pro if he could arrange a game for me with a person or persons who did not have a full group.

He told me of two gentlemen that had just gone down to the first tee and suggested I catch up with them as they are both new members and are also looking for a game. I caught up with them and introductions were made all the way around.

Knowing I was introduction challenged, I paid close attention and managed to remember that one of the gentlemen's name was Gord. I had no recollection of the second person's name.

As we walked off the tee I made a point of walking along with Gord and I asked him, "do you have any idea of the other's fellows name?"

"I'm not sure" he responded " but I think his name is Jim".

"Okay" I suggested, "let's call him Jim a couple of times and see what happens. If he responds, we're clean."

"Good idea" said Gord. "We'll go with that".

As we moved along, one or the other of us would say things like,

"Good shot, Jim."

"Your putt, Jim."

"I think this is your ball over here, Jim".

He always responded with a nod or a wave and Gord and I concluded that we had it right.

We had a delightful round and decided to buy each other a "pop" at the nineteenth hole and discuss whether or not we could put together another game.

We were sitting at the table when one of the members walked past, looked over and said, "Dave, how are you doing? I see your membership came through."

Gord and I looked at each other. The eyebrows went up.

"Who the hell is Dave?" I whispered to Gord.

"Beats me" he responded.

"That's me," said our friend Jim. He explained that as he had just met us, he didn't want to make an issue over the fact that neither of us got his name right so he felt he should just go along with answering to Jim. Some people are just way too polite.

Hi Mom!

I was asked by very good friends to propose the toast to the bride's mother at a wedding reception. It was fun to do and it gave me some extra insight into the relationship between mother and daughter.

It's said that fathers have a special place for daughters and daughters for their Dads, but in thinking about what to say that day I came to some startling realizations. It was a nice little speech and several people liked it. I've decided to include it among my stories I like to tell.

* * *

The wedding day of a daughter must be one of the proudest and yet, in a way, saddest days in a mother's life. When she sees her daughter dressed and coiffed as never before, when she knows the thoughtfulness that went into the selection of special items and jewellery, a mother's pride must be over-whelming.

She sees her daughter as a grown woman starting on a new life.

She also sees and remembers the little girl that needed her comfort when she was ill in the wee hours of the morning. She remembers the skinned knees. The tragedy that seemed about to spoil the prom dance until Mom fixed the loose thread. She remembers the talks over coffee when only the two of them sat at the kitchen table and worked things out. She remembers the report cards, the home made birthday cards, the Mother's Day breakfast in bed with the burnt toast and the egg that turned out scrambled.

She still sees her little girl, but she also sees a beautiful young woman with her proud husband sitting at her side.

Dads also take their little girls for walks. Dads also attend the concerts. Dads pay for the wardrobe and the school trips. Dads set up the education funds and cheer their daughters on when they win the race or receive the scholarship. Dads are there and join in the praise when their daughter gets her job and proudly brings home that first pay cheque. Dads also pick the kids up at school and drive them to the mall. Dads worry about late dates and new boyfriends.

But, as everyone of us knows, when that special moment of recognition is reached, when the award is given, when the spotlight goes on or the television camera is brought to focus for that special moment, every child and especially every daughter will look the camera straight in the eye and say,

"Hi Mom."

Raise a glass and offer that very special toast to Mom.

Happy New Year

Between 1968 and 2003 we have received thirty-five lumps of coal, thirty-five shortbread cookies and thirty-five pieces of silver coin. The total dollar cost value would be less than $15.00.

When we first moved to Jerseyville, we built our home next door to Jim and Flo. They had a trim white house, a garage that had been turned into a stable for his two horses and a yard full of various bits and pieces of old fashioned carriages and sleighs. They were good neighbours. Jim was of Scottish background but was born and raised in the area. Jim knew everyone and everyone knew Jim.

Jim became a collector of carriages and sleighs and also became a major restoration expert. He took it upon himself to research every carriage manufacturer throughout Southern Ontario and could tell you the history of almost every carriage shop that ever turned out four wheels and a bench. He trained his horses, Skip and Toby, to pull sleighs and wagons and became the hit of almost every Ancaster Heritage Day parade.

His restoration work wasn't without personal peril. During the summer months, he could work out in his garage/stable and clean, sand and paint to his heart's content. As the weather grew colder, he would quietly move one wheel at a time down into his basement and, before you knew it, there would be a complete carriage in the house. Flo took rather unkindly to that and before long a new barn and museum appeared in the back yard. That is now crammed with carriages, sleighs, lanterns, bells, bits and brasses that tell a large part of the travelling history of Ontario. If you have half an hour, Jim will gladly take three hours to give you a tour.

New Years had never been a big deal with me. We had gone through the party stage where it was mandatory that you had a little too much to drink and that you wear a funny hat and ring a bell at the stroke of twelve. I used to try to time a trip to the washroom so that I was out of the kissing firestorm that broke out at midnight. I'm not knocking the festivities. They just never turned my crank. I can't remember ever organizing a New Years Party. I can remember ducking more than a few.

Over the past several years we have joined three other couples and spent New Years in a most pleasurable way. Each year we go to a different house in the four couple rotation. The host sets a gourmet style dinner menu, designs and produces the menu, purchases the groceries and he and his three male companions proceed to prepare the meal while the ladies socialize and occasionally, ply us with drink. I've noticed, however, that the hostess for that evening is always very much on edge as she tries to deal with the thought that there are four male buffoons in her kitchen and that things may never be the same again.

The cooking and the organizing becomes the entertainment for the evening. Most times we are sitting down around nine o'clock and end up enjoying some surprisingly good dinners. We do manage to stay alert well past midnight but it is not an all night revelry with blinding headaches greeting the next day.

It's a good thing too. Apparently, there is an old Scottish belief that it's good luck if the first person to enter your home in the New Year is a dark-haired Scots person. The visitor is expected to bring a piece of coal for heat, a cookie or piece of bread for food and a piece of silver, signifying a wish for prosperity in the coming year.

Jim believes in the old tale so much that he finds himself thrown out of his own house just before midnight on New Years Eve so that he can be the first person to enter in the New Year. Flo, calling on her Scottish ancestry, sees to it.

We have moved three times since we built our house next to Jim and Flo. Every New Years Day since our first as their neighbours, Jim has appeared at our door as the first visitor of the year. The visits are a little later now than they once were. The chats and catch-ups are no less interesting and fun. It's a great visit.

We now have thirty-five lumps of coal, thirty-five pieces of shortbread and thirty-five pieces of silver. Only a complete fool would believe they have a value of only $15.00. Keep them coming, Jim. See you next year.